A Witch In Time

Book 3 , Magic and Mayhem

By

Robyn Peterman

DEDICATION

This book is for my mother-in-law, Zelda. I love your
name and I love you.

ACKNOWLEDGEMENTS

Writing books is the best job I've ever had. Sitting in my sweatpants, t-shirt, sparkly Uggs and no make-up totally works for me! However, as solitary as the writing process may be, putting a book out is a group effort. There are many important and wonderful people involved and I am blessed to have such a brilliant support system.

Rebecca Poole, your covers are perfect and you imagination delights me. Thank you.

Meg Weglarz, you save me from myself constantly with your editing. Thank you.

Donna McDonald, you are my partner in crime, one of my dearest friends and one hell of an author. I'd be in deep doodoo without you. Thank you.

Donna McDonald and JM Madden, you are the best and most honest critique partners a gal could have. I don't know what I would do without your eagle eyes and good taste. Thank you.

My beta readers; Wanda, Melissa, Susan and Karen, you rock so hard. Thank you.

Wanda, your organization skills keep me from going off the deep end. Thank you.

And my family... thank you for believing in me and understanding deadlines and my need to discuss fictional characters as if they were real people. None of this would be any fun without your love and support.

And my readers... I do this for you.

CHAPTER 1

"The paw is getting awfully close to the boob," I stated calmly, without taking my eyes from the TV. *Say Yes to The Dress* was on and it was a really good one. "If you value that fuzzy little arm, I'd remove it."

"Got no idea what you're bitchin' about, Dollface," Fat Bastard, my newly inherited wise-guy cat grumbled as he quickly removed the offending appendage from my chest.

He resituated himself on the couch, shoving his other two enormous and furry feline buddies over—Jango Fett and Boba Fett. Fat Bastard clearly needed a little more room to go to town on his nads.

Closing my eyes, I tried to block out the sound of three obese cats slurping on their no-nos, but alas, one didn't *hear* with the eyes. However, if I plugged my ears I would miss all the TV bridesmaids screaming in horror at the dress the gal was about to enter the room in. Forget the fact that I'd already seen the episode four times... Messing with my programs was not working for me.

"Don't you guys have something to do other than making me want to puke?" I asked as politely as I could considering I was seconds away from zapping their lazy asses off my couch.

"As your *familiars*, we wait for your orders," Boba said as he looked up and gave me a lopsided kitty grin.

If his back leg wasn't extended into a contorted position and his balls weren't flapping in the wind, it would have been cute... but this *following orders* thing was news to me. All witches had familiars—animals who were supposed to support and help their witch—or thwart in my case. I'd actually inherited the three idiots from my beloved, departed Aunt Hildy. They ate me out of house and home and ran an illegal gambling ring, but were excellent in a battle. Any magic shot at them simply bounced off and went back at the shooter. They'd actually saved my life and the lives of my friends recently so I was trying to deal with their obsessive cleaning habits.

"Wait. Are you serious? I can boss you around?"

"Nah," Jango grunted with a laugh. "He's just screwing with ya, Zelda."

I paused my show, glared at the overweight menagerie on my sofa and sighed. As much as it pained me, I kind of liked them—disgusting tendencies and all. Of course this was top-secret information I would only admit on my deathbed. I'd already admitted far too much to all of the new people in my life.

"Out," I snapped at the cats and pointed to the front door. "You fat dorks need some exercise. And if I catch any of you sleeping on the porch, I'll put you on the treadmill for an hour."

"We don't have no treadmill," Boba volunteered between licks.

I waved my hands in the air and a brand spanking new treadmill appeared in the foyer. I was only supposed to use my magic for the good of others, not to garner more TV time for myself. However, the cats were meaty and this was more for their good than mine.

"We do now," I informed them with a wicked little smile.

Their groans made me giggle.

"But I only have one section left," Fat Bastard complained, referring to his crotch.

"Move it or lose it," I said in a brook no catshit tone.

Slowly and apathetically they moseyed their bulbous butts off the couch and out the front door, whining all the way. Goddess, they were annoying.

"Damn." I moaned as I plopped back down on the now cat-free couch and realized I'd pressed the *off* button instead of the *pause* button on the remote. Whatever. I'd seen the episode before and knew the bride picked a heinous lacy dress because her grandma put her foot down. I didn't need to watch all that crap anyway. Furthermore, I was supposed to do thirty minutes a day of insightful meditation according to my new therapist, Roger the porno loving rabbit Shifter.

"What the hell does insightful meditation even mean?" I muttered to no one since I was blessedly alone for the first time in what felt like a week.

Closing my eyes and following the recommendation of the questionably skilled head- shrinker, I gave it a try. Of course the King of Shifters was the first image that crossed my mind. The gorgeous wolf shifter, Mac—all six foot four of sexy, dark haired, perfectly muscled, sapphire eyed, beautiful man. The very same one who was convinced I was his mate invaded my thoughts. I didn't believe the *mate* bullshit for a minute. I was a witch and he was a werewolf. A very good looking, hotter than hell werewolf who made me question my self-professed loner status. Constantly.

I closed my eyes and tried again. Not working.

"Hell, I'll just pretend I'm talking to someone about my pathetic, out of control existence," I announced to the empty room.

Still didn't work. I'd just save my meditation for therapy. A silent hour with Roger would drive him nuts.

"My dearest daughter," my dad called out as he walked in the front door and tripped over our new piece of furniture. "Your decorating skills leave a bit to be desired. Is there a reason we have a treadmill in the foyer?"

"The cats are fat," I explained logically.

"Yes, well, speaking of... I thought they were all having heart attacks. They're in an appalling pile just off the front porch panting like they've run a marathon."

"Good Goddess," I muttered with a giggle. "At least they made it off the porch. Where have you been?"

I was still getting used to having a parental unit and living with him. Fabio *slash* Naked Dude *slash* my dad was very new to my world. He hadn't known about me for most of my thirty years and had to pay a steep price to be back in my life once he found out I existed. It was complicated, but what in my life wasn't?

I stared at the beautiful man from whom I'd inherited my red hair and green eyes and grinned. I'd only recently started calling him Dad after he'd almost bitten the dust for the third time since we'd met. Near death experiences had a way with making me do things that were not in my normal repertoire—like caring for people.

My mom, who was cray-cray and didn't have a maternal bone in her body, had turned my Dad into a cat to punish him. He then, very sneakily, became my pain-in-the-ass familiar. And as the story goes... I accidentally ran over him with my car. Of course he came back from the dead since he was a freakin' cat with nine lives. However, he didn't rise from the dead until I'd served my nine months in the magical pokey for accidentally mowing his ass down.

The kicker was that I realized I loved him on his second kitty near-death catastrophe and apparently my love was the magic he needed to become a human again. Well, human was pushing it. He was a warlock with an unhealthy penchant for gambling. My dad was also an outstanding cook, procurer of designer clothes and he loved me. It was win-win-win.

In the beginning, I was sure he was using bad credit cards and stealing the outlandishly expensive duds for me. However, it turned out the old man was loaded. His fortune was questionably gained, but it made me feel much better about keeping all my dubious booty.

"I've joined the Town Council," Dad announced grandly as he waved his hand and made the treadmill disappear.

"Why did you do that?" I asked getting up off the couch and slapping my hands on my hips.

"Because if I'm going to live here, I need to have a say in the local politics. I'm fighting to have gambling legalized."

"Of course you are," I told him with an eye roll. "But I was talking about the treadmill. It was fine in the foyer."

"Zelda, those cats can barely make it to the front yard without passing out. You think they'll survive a round on a human walking machine?"

"Point," I agreed with a giggle. "However it was a good blackmail device."

"I'm sure it was," he agreed. "But I think a padlock on the refrigerator would suffice."

"Wrong," I countered with a shudder. "They have food stashed all over the house so they won't starve."

"Are they planning on eliminating all the mice we're going to attract by turning our home into a two story grocery store?" Dad inquired as he dropped a few high-end shopping bags on the coffee table.

"They're keeping them as pets." I sidled closer to the bags. "Are those for me?"

Nordstrom, Neiman and Fleur of England—my dad had taste far superior to any woman I knew.

"That depends," he answered coyly as he stepped between my hands and the treasures on the table.

"Depends on what?" I asked with narrowed eyes. He had ways of getting me to do things that I had no intention of doing. Cashmere was his evil weapon... and Prada... and Gucci and the list went on and on.

Yes, I was materialistic, but I was getting a grip on it. Part of my maturity or more accurately, my parole, was that I could only use my magic for the good of others. Therefore, I was now unable conjure up shoes that cost more than most people made in six months. It was difficult, but doable thus far. Dad's excessive shopping habits helped tremendously.

If I was being honest, I felt better about using my power for others—not that I would let it be known. My reputation as an uncaring, selfish, irresponsible witch was getting seriously tarnished here. The Shifters in Assjacket, West Virginia thought I was a good and compassionate witch. Being thought of kindly was taking some getting used to and I kept waiting for the other shoe to drop—it always did.

But back to the matter at hand.

"Depends on what?" I repeated, not liking the smirk on my father's face.

My dad, Fabio was a crafty sucker. How did I know? I was cut from the same cloth.

"Well, it's a funny story," he started as he got comfortable on the couch next to me.

"Funny as in *ha-ha* or funny as in *oh my Goddess are you freakin' serious*?" I asked, trying to peek inside the bags.

Dad paused and scratched his head as he considered his answer. This did not bode well. If he had to come up with a story I would find palatable, we were in trouble before we began and I sooooooo wanted what was inside the bags. Damn.

"I suppose a bit of both," he conceded as he pushed the bags farther away, but not without revealing some of the contents first.

My breath caught in my throat as I spied a very expensive purse I'd been eyeing and *of course* some cashmere. He was a total butthole.

"Out with it," I snapped wanting to find out if I had to deny the bribe on the table. I really didn't want to, but my dad's hemming and hawing was making me uneasy.

"So I applied for a position and they don't want me to have it," he huffed and threw his hands in the air. "It's just not fair."

"Was it Town Treasurer?" I asked with a snicker.

My dad's finessing of finances made the good folks of Assjacket a little wary—and with good reason. He was the BIG winner at my cat's illegal gambling ring and from what I'd heard everyone in town owed him money.

"No, although that would have been a smart move on their part. I could raise millions for this area. All we need is a casino and a few well heeled out of town guests," he pondered aloud with an evil gleam in his eye. "Maybe a horse track... "

"Bad idea," I said redirecting my flighty father. "Let's get back to the story that involves me tearing into the packages on the table."

"Right," he agreed and clapped his hands together twice. "I've applied to be the artistic director of the community theatre."

"Whoa, there are so many weird things about that statement I'm not sure where to start."

He gave me an *I'm going to ground you* stare and pressed his fingers to his temples. "You're supposed to be on my side," he pointed out.

"I am," I insisted, "especially when there are bags involved. But what kind of place puts the artistic director of a dinky ass community theatre on the Town Council?"

"Assjacket," he shot back with a grin.

My newly adopted town wasn't really called Assjacket, but it was how I referred to it. The new name was catching on, much to the displeasure of the older Shifters in our community. I also referred to my job as the Shifter Wanker, formerly known as the Shifter Whisperer. Wanker fit me better. I was a healer who could talk with the Shifters in their animal form. Not my first choice of vocation, but since I hadn't come up with anything better or less life threatening, I took the post.

I was good at it even though it hurt like a mother humper to heal the clumsy idiots. I secretly loved my job—not the pain—the job.

"Okay, I'll bite. Why won't they let you be the *artistic director?*"

"They consider me high risk since I'm not a Shifter," he pouted.

"What about community theatre is risky at all?" I asked perplexed. "I mean, my Goddess, you would costume the hell out of any show you did."

"Right?" he grumbled in agreement. "I told them this, but apparently Assjacket's thespian society is the laughing stock of West Virginia."

"First of all, never say the world thespian again. And secondly, because I enjoy asking questions that I don't want the answers to... why?"

Dad's grin was positively contagious and my own grin pulled at my lips in response.

"The last show they produced was a musical version of *Silence of the Lambs.* Several audience members got eaten and the Fava Bean number was lewd," he replied trying desperately not to laugh.

"Bullshit." I slapped my hands over my mouth as I too tried not to laugh. Eating paying customers was *not* funny. "You're making that up," I accused through splayed fingers.

"How could I even begin to make something like that up?" he demanded, insulted that I would doubt him. "The disaster before that was a musical version of *Friday the 13ᵗʰ*."

Fabio, my several centuries old *father figure* of questionable maturity, could hold back no longer. He fell to the floor and laughed so hard tears streamed from his eyes. He could barely breathe. I was now convinced this horrific story was true... which was why I was appalled and furious with myself that I was in hysterics too.

"Did anyone die during that one?" I squeaked, hating myself with each request for more details.

"No," he choked out, as he wiped his eyes and admirably attempted to pull himself together. "A few stab wounds."

"Wait," I said as I punched his arm. "When you say eaten do you mean *eaten*?"

"Yesssssss," he hissed back in hysterics. "But it was only a hand and a foot if I'm remembering correctly."

I heaved a huge sigh of relief coupled with a gag. I'd envisioned total cannibalism.

"Thank Goddess," I grunted. "Wait, I'm confused."

"About the Fava Bean number?" he asked with an enormous grin.

"Um... no—absolutely not. Those are three more words you shall never utter again. About the bribe bags on the table."

"Ahhh," he said as he got back up to his feet and began placing the contents of the bags on the table inches from my fingers. "There's a caveat."

"And that would be?" I asked as I closed my eyes when he plopped a rockin' pair of Jimmy Choo pumps on the table next to an obscene pile of green cashmere that matched my eyes perfectly.

"They'll let me have the job if you agree to star in the next show."

My dad was a dick of epic proportions. I was not an actress. I couldn't sing to save my life and I wasn't going to have any part of a life threatening musical no matter how much I coveted the booty on the table.

"Nope," I said with my eyes squeezed shut so hard I felt a headache coming on.

"Come on Zelda," Dad pleaded.

I could hear him placing more items on the table and I was seconds away from shrinking the clothing on his body to extra small. This was so unfair.

"You listen to me," I hissed as I sat on my hands and kept my eyes firmly closed. It was too risky to have the use of my hands. I'd either zap him, which wasn't nice, or I'd grab the stash on the table and run. Neither scenario was attractive or happening. "I'm a witch who heals dumb ass Shifters when they get booboos. I do not have the time to humiliate myself in front of the masses on stage. I do fine with that in my daily life. The answer is a big, fat, hairy no."

"All right then." He sighed dramatically. "I suppose Sassy might like the black Hermes Birkin bag with the gold hardware."

"Do you hate me?" I shouted as I threw myself over the bag like it was a fumbled football in the Super Bowl. "Sassy's coloring does not go with this bag. It would look much better carried by someone with red hair. And you're a total dick."

"I've been called far worse," he replied with a chuckle and then sighed dramatically. "All of this is yours. I was just hoping you would humor an old warlock. I so wanted to be in charge of an extravaganza."

He gently pried me off of the bag and placed it in my arms along with all the other apparel. I stared down at my windfall and wanted to cry. Dad sat down next to me and put his head in his hands... and he wasn't trying to trick me anymore. Shit.

"I don't need this stuff. You can give the bag to Saaaa... ssaaay," I whispered as I felt the need to either put my head between my knees or breathe into a paper bag. "You have to stop spending money on me. I don't deserve any of it. I called you a dick. I'm pretty sure daughters calling their fathers dicks isn't good."

"No, no, it's fine," he assured me as he put his arms around me and squeezed. "I wasn't there for your teenage years so you owe me about four years of calling me a dick."

"Only four?" I asked with a small grin.

"Okay, five," Dad conceded generously with an adorable lopsided grin.

We sat in silence for a few minutes. It felt so nice to be held by him. I was thirty, but in his arms I was a little girl—a wanted and adored little girl.

"I can't believe I'm going to say this... but I'll think about it," I muttered as I shook my head in defeat. "However, I refuse to sing or dance or talk that much."

"I can work with that," he promised with a smile that lit his whole face.

"What's the show?" I asked as I played with the clasp on my brand new, ridiculously overpriced purse.

"It's a surprise. I don't even know. Bob the beaver and Roger the rabbit are writing it," he said as he absently smoothed my hair back.

"Holy hell, that sounds dangerous. Roger's a perv. If he writes a song and dance filled *Debbie Does Dallas*, I'm out."

"Me too," Dad agreed with a laugh and a shudder. "Let's just wait and see what they come up with. It might be fun and we'll get to spend some real quality time together."

Famous last words.

CHAPTER 2

"No, no, no, I'm not *writing* the show. I'm the set designer," Roger the rabbit Shifter *slash* my therapist assured me with a doctor-ly chuckle. "Bob the beaver writes all the shows."

"Did he write the last two?" I inquired with raised brows as I made myself comfortable on Roger's offensively plaid office couch.

"Um... yes," he whispered and blanched. "Those were dark times for Bob."

"And the people who got eaten and stabbed? I'm guessing those were dark times for them too?" I added as I pinched the bridge of my nose and winced.

"Well, yes. We had quite a few lawsuits on our hands. The Town Treasury went bankrupt after those very unfortunate incidents," he replied as he scrubbed his hands over his face. "Thankfully, your dearly departed Aunt Hildy was able to heal most of the victims."

My Aunt Hildy had been the Shifter Whisperer before me. She was gone now and I owned the job—or rather, the job owned me.

"So what would you like to talk about today?" Roger inquired carefully, as I was here for a session.

He was terrified of me. This was a good thing. I'd randomly discovered his porn addiction much to the

17

displeasure of my over-active gag reflex, but it kept us on an even keel. Hippocratic Oath be damned. If the little turd gossiped about our sessions, I'd reveal his penchant for watching people hump. Win-win.

I didn't want to do our sessions, but I'd lost a bet to my dad and had to visit with Roger too many times to count—nine to be exact and thank the Goddess I'd already done one. I'd suggested we do them all in one day, but Roger almost had a coronary. Since I was the one who would have to heal the little shit if his ticker blew up, I generously agreed to twice a week—on different days.

"I was thinking you could watch me meditate for an hour," I explained, getting into a yoga position and winking at him.

"Zelda." His forehead furrowed and his nose twitched.

Damn, he looked like a rabbit even in his human form.

"Roger," I shot back imitating his stern tone.

"Fine." He gave up and shrugged. "Why don't we just chat about things that won't help you grow as a person or get over your fear of abandonment or make you realize you're a lovable person?"

"Sounds good to me," I said wanting to throw one of his big head-shrinker books at his face.

We sat in silence for a few minutes while I watched Roger rack his brain for a subject that would keep him safe from my itchy magical fingers.

"I have to say, I'm very excited that you've agreed to star in the show."

He chose the wrong topic of conversation.

"Um… Dude—may I call you Dude?" I snapped sarcastically, not waiting for a reply. "I have agreed to nothing. Nothing. I want no part of a theatrical production where innocent by-standers bleed profusely."

"I see," Roger stated and jotted a few notes on a pad.

"What did you just write?" I demanded as I tried to peek at his notebook.

Roger eyed me for a long moment and I squirmed a bit in my seat.

"Fear of success," he said sadly. "Fear of mass adulation. Fear of love."

"Did you drink before our session?" I asked as my eyes grew large and the need to smack his head off his shoulders consumed me.

"It's only two o'clock." Roger checked his watch and nodded with satisfaction. "I never drink before four."

"Good to know." I made a silent promise to myself to check the session times of my future appointments with the good doctor. "I'm not doing the show. I told Fabio I would think about it. And the *only* reason I'm considering it is because Fabio wants to fit into Assjacket and it might help curb his gambling hobby."

"I thought you were calling him Dad now," Roger noted with surprise.

"I am," I hissed. "I just wanted to be sure you knew who I was talking about."

"Right." His brows rose as he scribbled some more crap on his pad.

"Fine," I shouted as Roger jumped in terror and his pad flew over his head. "You win. I'll talk about all the painful and embarrassing stuff you want me to puke up. You happy now?"

"Only if you are," Roger stated calmly as he hopped off his chair and placed a bucket at my feet.

I stared at it for a moment and then laughed. "That was a metaphor. I'm not going to really hurl."

"My bad," Roger apologized as he quickly retrieved the pail and sat back down.

Again we sat in silence staring at each other.

"Why don't we pretend this is our first session and you get me up to speed on the last few months," he suggested.

"I thought I wasn't supposed to pretend in here," I said, trying to figure out how to get out of what I'd just committed myself to.

"It's a game," he replied evenly. "Just go with it."

"Whatever." I uncrossed my legs and grabbed a pillow from the couch. I squeezed it tight to my chest and took a deep breath. I knew I needed to try here. Roger might be a perv, but everyone I trusted in town swore he was a great therapist.

"My name is Zelda and um… I'm a witch with a few minor-ish problems. I really don't want to be here, but since I have outstanding blackmail information on you, I feel fairly confident that what's said in the office, stays in the office."

He nodded and smiled. It was a real smile and I felt a tiny bit bad for giving him so much shit, but this was difficult for me. However, I wasn't a weenie or a quitter. I was a semi-out-of-control witch with issues who needed to deal with said issues. I could do this. Maybe.

"Soooooo, Roger, the last year has been a doozy. I spent nine months in the stanky magic pokey for killing my cat who miraculously rose from the dead and turned out to be my dad. Interesting coincidence. To be fair to me, it was a total accident," I said as my eyes narrowed at Roger while I waited for his reaction.

"Accident, you say?" he questioned with a partially raised left brow.

"I know it looks bad since I didn't like the mangy little son of a bitch, but I'm a healer not a killer," I insisted.

"When I heard the first crunch I'd freaked out so much that I hit reverse and drive simultaneously a few times before I got out of my car and screamed bloody murder. So as you can see it *was* an accident. However, to make things right, I buried Fabio in a new Prada shoebox and left the super soft shoe bags inside as a blanket and a pillow. After Naked Dude's—or Dad as I now call him—resurrection, he complimented me on his cozy coffin."

"That was a lovely touch," Roger agreed making me like him a little more.

"Thank you, I thought so."

"Welcome," he replied warmly. "Let's continue."

I ran my hands through my wild red hair and groaned. This was ridiculous and I was losing it, but I wasn't a quitter—twenty-two minutes to go.

"Of course, it didn't matter to Baba Yaga, the most powerful and horrendously dressed witch in existence, that it had been an accident or that my cat *slash* dad had actually lived. I had to serve time in the pokey with a heinous cellmate, Sassy the Violent Witch from Hell who now, much to my horror, is my neighbor in Assjacket. And on top of *that* shit show, Baba Yonutbag is apparently dating my dad," I told my head shrinker.

"Do you have a problem with your dad dating?" he queried, supplying the normal therapist response to a child mentioning a parent was seeing someone.

"Nope. He's a big boy and can make his own mistakes."

The rabbit said nothing—just smiled and made some more notes.

I groaned and wondered if there was a straight jacket somewhere in the office that I could put on. Nope, no straight jacket... I let several minutes tick by feigning deep thought. When it reached really awkward silence I started talking again.

"After my release, I found out about Aunt Hildy who left me her house—a dead aunt I never knew. My task ended up being avenging her, taking over her job as the Shifter Whisper and maintaining the magical balance in Assjacket, West Virginia—far easier said than done. You idiots are violent."

Roger bobbed his head politely in agreement.

Pacing would help me blow through the rest of my recent history faster. Sitting was making me itchy or maybe it was that I was getting to the parts I didn't like. Standing up and tossing the pillow on the couch, I jogged the perimeter of the room and refused to make eye contact with my porno-loving therapist.

"Anyhoo, my beautiful and very dead Aunt Hildy came back as a ghost and was instrumental in helping save the day. She's gone now, as you know. I wanted her to stay with me," I said quietly and slowed my pace. "She's gone on to the Next Adventure with her mate, Chuck the bear Shifter, who died in the magical battle with the honey badgers."

The battle that had been the fault of my mother…

My mother was one of the main reasons I needed therapy. Her lack of any maternal instinct and her attempts at killing me kind of screwed with my chi, not to mention my self-worth. It also made me wary of relationships and believing people loved me. Blahblahblah.

I liked to think of it as water under the bridge especially since I'd very recently turned my mother into a mortal. She was now incapable of hurting anyone ever again. Or so I'd thought… Therapy was a bitch and teaching me I hadn't quite let go of the unwanted, unloved little girl I used to be—or still was.

"This sucks," I muttered as I checked the clock on the wall. Shit, fifteen more minutes to go. I was a witch of my word so I resumed my pacing and dove back in.

"If this is too difficult we can talk about something else," Roger offered kindly.

"I'm not a weenie."

"Never said you were," he replied, cowering a little.

"I can do this," I said as I curbed my need for movement and sat back down on the couch. "You really should get a more attractive couch."

"So noted," he said with a chuckle.

"I can help you shop for that," I volunteered in a pathetic attempt to steer the subject toward buying stuff—something I enjoyed greatly.

"I'd like that."

Fourteen and a quarter minutes to go. He didn't fall for the diversion tactic. Crap.

"Sooooo, my mission or parole requirement thanks to Baba Yodumbass was to become the new Shifter Whisperer—or Shifter Wanker as I prefer to go by. Coming from a rare line of healers, my job makes unfortunate sense. I've never stayed anywhere very long and have few friends to show for it. Sassy does *not* count. She's insane and ruined my favorite jeans. Belonging somewhere is new to me and it makes me happy which is not good. So, I refuse to get used to it. I'm a survivor and have gone most of my life as a loner. Less messy that way."

"Messy is what showers and therapy are for," Roger volunteered quietly.

"That was kind of profound," I said surprised.

"Yes, well, I did go to medical school." His lips were pursed and his eyes twinkled.

"I should hope so," I shot back with a laugh. "I kind of figured you might have done it on line in between watching your *shows*."

"My shows also inform my profession," Roger explained.

"You moonlight as a hooker?"

"Um... no. I'm also a sexual therapist," he reminded me. "Which brings me to Mac and you."

"Mac and I do just fine in the sack," I told him, offended that he would think otherwise.

"I'm sure you do, but do you think it's wise to let that be the lynch pin of your relationship?"

"Would you like me to lynch pin your head to your desk?" I inquired, willing myself not to zap his ass into tomorrow.

"No, that sounds rather unpleasant," he stated weakly as he wrung his hands. "I was simply suggesting that because you're each other's mates, you spend some quality time truly getting to know each other without the physical getting in the way."

"The physical is *not* in the way. And we're not mates."

Roger just stared at me. I liked it better when he said stupid stuff and I could jump down his bunny throat. This silence stuff was unnerving.

"Okay, then," he said in a reasonable doctor tone. "How many relationships with men have you had where you could tell me details other than sexual?"

Shitballs. He had me there. I decided to answer him with his own freaky medicine. I stayed mute. Unfortunately, so did he.

After about a twelve-ish minute stare down, he'd clearly had enough. "Would you like to talk about your mother?" he proposed gamely.

"I'd *love* to, but it looks like our time is up for this enlightening and nauseating session."

As I peeked at the clock, I heaved a sigh of relief. I'd tortured myself and Roger with my history for a full session. That was enough.

"I'll see you next time," Roger said with a smile and a nod.

"I'd say thank you but I'd be lying. I'm pretty sure you want me to be truthful in here," I said knowing I was being rude, but unable to stop myself. Roger didn't deserve my disrespect. He was truly trying to help. However, I needed to *accept* it and my attitude was a little sucky. Well, there was always next time...

"Zelda, it's all going to be okay. I believe that and I wish you would too."

I looked down at my hands and screwed my eyes shut so no tears fell. Roger was wrong. I wanted him to be right, but I'd learned a long time ago that good stuff was always temporary for me. I wanted to stay in Assjacket. For the first time in my life I felt part of something bigger than just myself. I knew I should cut my losses and run while they all still liked me.

However, with a newly found father, a *boyfriend*—for lack of a better word, and a town full of Shifters I was getting far too attached to, it was hard to leave. So I was here, at least for the moment. I'd promised Mac eight more dates before I blew this joint and I was keeping my word. It would make it more painful to leave when the time came, but a promise was a promise.

"Um... Thank you," I mumbled as I high tailed it to the door. "I'll see you in two days."

Bizarrely, I did feel a little better—more confused, but better.

Maybe the pervy rabbit was onto something.

CHAPTER 3

I left Roger's office in a full out sprint and came to a dead halt when I spotted the gorgeous man leaning on his motorcycle across the street—the very same man who was convinced beyond a doubt that I belonged to him and visa-versa. He was the sexiest distraction I'd ever seen—six foot four, wavy chocolate brown hair, sapphire blue eyes and an ass you could bounce a quarter off of... not to mention a face that would make angels weep.

His sexy smirk made my knees weak and the need to jump his bones went all through me. However, Roger's stupid words were still sitting at the forefront of my brain. Damn that rabbit.

"Are you stalking me?" I asked with a grin as I approached warily. I wasn't worried about his actions. I was concerned with mine. Getting arrested for public indecency wasn't on my agenda today.

"Possibly," Mac said studying me with unabashed appreciation. "How'd it go with Roger?"

"He thinks we shouldn't have sex."

The look on Mac's face was priceless, but the next part not so much.

"Babe, would you mind watching my bike for a minute?" he asked calmly—too calmly.

"Um... sure. Why?"

"I just need to go and beat the hell out of Roger. Won't take long," he promised as he started toward Roger's office.

"No," I shouted. "If anyone gets to beat Roger up it's me and I didn't tell you the whole story."

"Talk fast," he said tersely as he ran his hands through his hair. "Otherwise, Roger has an ass-kicking coming."

"Okay... um, he said I use sex to escape real emotion and since we're mates, which I still call bullshit on, I need to know you on more than just a biblical level. He said sex might be getting in the way of us forging a deeper relationship."

"He said all that?" Mac asked with surprise as his body relaxed somewhat.

"Well, kind of. He implied some crap and then I pieced the rest together," I admitted sheepishly.

"What do you think about that?" Mac walked back over and took my hand in his.

It was warm and felt so right—but right didn't last.

"Um... I think Roger is a perv and you know, I'm not sure he really even has a degree. There's a big ass diploma on the wall, but that doesn't mean much... Knowing everything about a person is usually unpleasant. I mean, I don't want to know about your past gal-pals because I'd have to kill them. Since you're older than dirt that would mean a lot of killing on my part. Just having left the pokey, I really don't want to go back any time soon—it sucked... and um... emotion isn't really my thing, so screwing works. Roger is a douchewagon," I finished very un-eloquently.

"Roger is right," he said.

"Wait. What?"

"The rabbit is right," Mac repeated firmly.

"You're not going to kick his furry rabbit ass?"

27

"Not today."

What the hell had I just done?

"Bon Jovi doesn't want to have sex with me?" I asked, shocked.

"Bon Jovi *definitely* wants to have sex with you," he said, referring to his obviously erect man part by the name I'd given it. "However, I want you forever and if getting into your heart means staying out of your pants, I'm all for it."

"My Little Red Riding Hood is not happy about this. At all."

"We'll have sex again when we mate," he informed me watching carefully for my reaction.

"Whoa, buddy. That's blackmail," I shot back with narrowed eyes and a few sparks flying from my very unhappy fingertips. "And I haven't agreed to anything."

"Desperate times call for desperate measures," he replied silkily. "Case in point... I'm willingly calling my Johnson by the emasculating name Bon Jovi."

"Johnson is a terrible name for a wiener."

"Nope," he disagreed with a wince. "Wiener is a terrible name for a Johnson *or* a Bon Jovi. I *do not* have a wiener. I have a mammoth... "

"Ego?" I supplied.

"Yes. And dick."

I couldn't disagree with that. He did and he knew how to use it. Shitshitshit. Me and my big mouth.

"So pretty girl, you ready for number eight?" he asked as he pulled me down Main Street.

"Is that a date or a sexual position?" I inquired grumpily as I let him drag me down the street.

"Date. We're going to improvise," he replied as he covertly adjusted the crotch his jeans.

"What were we going to do before our new vow of celibacy?" I inquired as I copped a feel of his ass, happy that his balls were probably turning blue.

"I was going to take you out to the tree fort I built in the woods this morning and play Rapunzel. I was going to climb your hair and then do you till you couldn't walk," Mac replied as casually as if he said the sky is blue.

"Stop," I shouted, yanking him to a halt. I inhaled deeply through my nose and blew it out through my lips. Hyperventilating or passing out was not attractive. I held on to him for purchase and willed myself not to shake. "You built me a tree house?"

"I did."

By his alarmed expression it was clear he wasn't sure if that was a good thing or a bad thing.

"Nobody ever built me a tree house," I said quietly, sucking back my ever-present tears. Sex till I couldn't walk was awesome, but a tree house... for me?

Mac took me in his arms and held me tight. "I'll build you a tree village if that would make you happy," he whispered into my hair.

"You're not playing fair," I accused.

"Nope. Fair is for losers. I plan to win," he said cockily as he placed his hand under my chin and raised my eyes to his. "How am I doing?"

I closed my eyes. His serious expression was telling me a story I wasn't ready to hear. Mac didn't know me like I knew me. He deserved far better than me—he was the freakin' King. I was *not* a Queen.

"I'm insane," I told him bluntly, avoiding the answer to his question. "I've never maintained a relationship or friendship in my life for more than two weeks. I'm a bed hog and I'll stab you with a fork if you take the last piece of cake." I sucked in some air and kept going. It would be far easier if he would just walk away now. I didn't necessarily want to, but I knew I could speed the process with the ugly truth. "I'm a butthole during my time of the month and a butthole on other random occasions as well. I despise being late and will do damage to your Bon Jovi if you're tardy. I have a potty mouth and will probably be a horrid mother to anything that I would blow out of my hooha. And I'm really bad with puppies."

"You done?" he asked.

"No. I'm not. Since no one can give me evidence that I wouldn't have a litter of tiny furry things with you, I see this as an insurmountable problem. Also the *mate biting* thing still skeeves me out. I'm not really into pain except for a little spanky-spanky every now and then. Your teeth are sharp when you pop fang and while I find that stupidly hot, I'm not really down with you sinking them into me."

"Done now?"

His entire face was smiling. *What the Hell?* He was supposed to be running in the opposite direction. What was wrong with him?

"A few more things," I snapped in frustration.

"Go ahead."

He pulled us over to a park bench and got comfortable. His half smirk of enjoyment made me want to deck him. I was freakin' serious. I suppose he thought he was in for a long one by the way he lounged back and waited patiently. Smart man.

"I watch reality TV and sing in the shower. I'm tone deaf and this has scared and scarred many people. Fabio and the cats have earplugs stashed all over the house. I have no plans to end my vocal hobby and bleeding eardrums hurt. I... um, can't cook and I'll eat you out of house and home. My metabolism is awesome and as long as it stays that way I'll eat my own weight in cookies daily. And… well, I… " Shit, I was running out of stuff. "You need a sophisticated woman to be your Queen."

"May I speak?" Mac asked calmly.

"Okay," I replied cautiously. As much as I knew the big break up was inevitable, a huge part of me didn't want it to be today… or ever.

"Everyone is crazy. We all just wear it differently. Some you can see and some is disguised. I don't trust anyone who's not at least a little insane, so you're fine on that point. As far as the two week moratorium on relationships, we're already way past that. We've been together almost two months. I win," he informed me smugly.

"But… "

"My turn," Mac reminded me as he gently put his finger over my lips. "You can hog my bed any time you want. I like cake, but the last piece shall always be yours as long as I always get the last bite of steak. I'd rather tolerate you being a butthole than deal with anyone else's shit in the world—vaguely gross pun intended. I'm always punctual, barring having to kill someone or saving the town, and I think your potty mouth is hot."

Again I tried to counter. Again he pressed his finger to my mouth. I was torn between biting it and sucking on it.

With a wide grin he continued. "It's true that a witch and a wolf haven't mated before, but all Shifters are born in human form. We don't shift until our second birthday so I'm confident you won't blow out puppies. I can guarantee you will change you mind about the *bite*, but we can always tie one on to relax you before we get down to business. Not wasted, mind you—just a little tipsy to take the edge off."

"How about unconscious?" I suggested and then slapped my hand over my mouth. Why in the hell was I suggesting anything having to do with mating?

His laugh was sexy and went right to my girly parts. I rolled my eyes and tried not to smile—impossible.

"You definitely wouldn't want to be knocked out for the bite because seconds after we mate we'll go into what's called Mating Frenzy. Do I need to spell that one out for you?" he inquired politely with a gleam in his eyes.

"Um, no. I'm good," I choked out. Goddess, I wanted to tackle him and ride him like a bronco.

"Also, I'd like to point out I find it very flattering that you find my fangs hot. My dick gets hard every time your hands light up like fireworks."

"That's a little weird," I commented, secretly delighted.

"Yep," he agreed with a huge grin.

"You done?"

"Nope, a few more points to cover," he said sounding like a lawyer winning a career making case. "The remote will be yours as long you watch TV naked. This is nonnegotiable. And you'll be delighted, or possibly appalled, to know that I too am tone deaf and will happily sing duets with you. It'll keep visitors away and give us far more time for sex—my favorite hobby. Jeeves cooks and I'm loaded, so the grocery bill is not an issue."

"You forgot one," I said quietly, knowing it was a big point.

"No. I didn't."

"I'm not a Queen."

He looked at me long and hard. I desperately wanted to glance away because I knew what was coming. It was unavoidable, but I was trapped in his beautifully intense stare.

"You're *my* Queen. You're everything I've ever wanted and I've waited for you my entire long life. All I need my Queen to do is love me back."

And there was the million-dollar question. Could I love him like he deserved to be loved? I still wasn't sure what love really meant. I was pretty sure I loved Fabio *slash* Dad, but that was the natural order of things. Children were supposed to love their parents. And that was also the conundrum. My life didn't follow natural order—at all. My mother didn't love me. Her failed attempt at killing me put all hopes of a healthy normal mother-daughter relationship to rest.

"Mac, I… "

"Nope," he whispered. "No more words on this particular subject right now. I have a handful of dates left before you're allowed to make any kind of decision. We clear?"

"Bossy much?" I said, relieved to have gotten a pass for the moment.

"I'm an alpha werewolf who never loses. What did you expect?" he shot back with a laugh.

I squinted my eyes at him and bit down on my lip so I didn't grin. "Are we really not going to play hide the salami?"

His pained groan made me giggle. "Do not call my Bon Jovi a salami—ever. And no, we're not. Roger, damn him to hell, is correct."

"What about making out and a little dry humpy-humpy?" I offered as a conciliation prize.

I watched him consider my suggestion. Again he had to adjust his jeans.

"I suppose that could work," he pondered aloud with some hesitation.

"How about a BJ?"

"No. As much as it pains me, and let me make it *very* clear that it pains me," he said referring to the large bulge in his pants. "We can't take off our clothes."

"No kisses for Bon Jovi?" I teased.

"Killing me here," he grunted as he looked to the heavens and appeared to be praying to the Goddess for strength.

"Fine," I muttered on a sigh. "We won't be able to stick to it anyway."

"Is that a challenge?" His brows arched and his grin widened.

"No, it's a fact," I replied cockily. "We haven't gone a day since we met without doing the nasty."

"You should know far better than daring me, little girl."

"Ohhhhh," I said with a mock shiver of fear and a giggle. "The Big Bad Wolf likes a challenge?"

"The Big Bad Wolf likes you. I'd say he *definitely* likes a challenge," he replied easily as he scooped me up into his strong arms and marched us down the street.

"You're a dork," I squealed as I kind-of, sort-of, not really tried to escape his hold.

His laugh made my heart light—scary but nice.

"I've been called worse. You hungry?"

"Dumb question. I'm always hungry." I snuggled in closer and went along for the ride.

"Good. I'm taking you to lunch."

"You gonna eat me?" I inquired, rubbing against him like a cat in heat. I knew I wasn't playing fair, but the new rules were frightening. Physical I could handle. Emotional? I wasn't so sure…

"You're cheating," he said, squeezing my ass and making my game backfire.

"Okay, okay," I huffed, giving up for the moment. "Hands off the ass unless you want me to zap you naked and take advantage of you on Main Street. I'll agree to no sex… for today. Where are we going to lunch?"

"To the diner."

"Assjacket has a diner?" I asked totally surprised. Why didn't I know this?

"Assjacket has a diner," he assured me as we approached a dilapidated old house.

"Oh my hell," I muttered as I took in the crumbling building. "This is the diner?"

"Yep," he said with a smirk. "Don't judge a book by its cover."

As with the rest of my life lately, he was correct. Very little was as it seemed.

CHAPTER 4

Everything in Assjacket was made to look horrible on the outside so the humans stayed away. People just drove right on through thinking the little one street town was just a rundown slum. The local Shifters couldn't have been happier about the misconception. What the humans didn't realize was within the decaying crumbling walls was magic—pure unadulterated magic.

Case in point—the Assjacket Diner.

"Oh my Goddess," I gasped as I took in the charming decor and the delicious aromas. "Totally amazing."

"Welcome to my humble place of business," Wanda the lovely raccoon Shifter greeted Mac and me with hugs as he put me down on my feet. "I was wondering when you'd make time to come by."

"If I'd known it existed I would have been living here," I told her as I wandered over to the pastry display. "Is that cheesecake?" I squealed.

"My *famous* cheesecake," Wanda informed me proudly with a sweet blush and a laugh. "You two go get a booth and DeeDee will be right over to get your order."

As Mac and I made our way to a cozy booth I waved at my Shifter friends—many of whom I'd healed. The diner was full of every animal you could think of happily chatting and eating, thankfully most of them in their human forms. My kind of place—especially the eating part.

The tables were all a heavy dark wood and covered in charming Shabby Chic-ish tablecloths and kitschy mismatched napkins. Floral teacups and saucers like a grandma should have sat atop the tables and screamed for the patrons to drink from them with an extended pinkie. It was all kinds of awesome.

"This place is Wanda's?" I asked Mac as I greedily perused the menu.

"It belongs to Wanda and DeeDee," he told me as he watched me with amusement. "Jeeves is now the head chef."

"You're shitting me." I clapped my hands together in glee and a huge grin split my face. Jeeves could cook.

"Do I look like I'm shitting you?" Mac chuckled and shook his head.

Jeeves was a very rare and extremely weird kangaroo Shifter. Decades ago on a vacation to Australia, Mac had found the young joey dying on the side of the road and adopted him so he would be under his protection. Jeeves was a misfit personified who was strangely adorable and could cook like a professional chef.

But there were two major downsides—Jeeves still lived at home with Mac and was dating my ex-cellmate and royal pain in my ass, Sassy. Sassy was a witch with an attitude problem who was now claiming to be my best friend. This was patently untrue, but once she got an idea in her pea-sized brain there was no changing it.

Sassy had been helpful during the last battle as one of her gifts was getting into peoples' heads and reading minds, but she was a magical menace and she was everywhere.

"DeeDee's busy doing some kind of deer Shifter shit, so you get meeeeeeeeee!" the bane of my existence screeched at decibels that belonged outside.

"Who did I screw over in a former life that I can't get away from you?" I asked wearily as I looked up from the menu and gasped in outraged shock at Sassy's attire. "Tell me that's not my baby blue cashmere cardigan that your obscenely large boobs are stretching out."

"Okay," she said with a casual shrug and no eye contact whatsoever. "It's not your baby blue cashmere sweater that my mind bogglingly sexy knockers are filling out beautifully."

"Yes it is," I hissed as my fingers began to spark. I was so done with her pilfering my clothes and then returning them either stained or stretched out beyond recognition.

"Of course it's yours," she said with an enormous eye roll. "But you told me to tell you it wasn't."

"It was a figure of speech," I ground out, wondering if Wanda and DeeDee would be upset if I set Sassy's hair on fire for a few minutes.

"Dude," she said with another eye roll that beat her previous one. "I did not take French in high school. If you want to be understood you need to speak English."

"Are you serious?" I yelled in my own outdoor voice.

"I believe she is," my good buddy Simon the skunk Shifter said from the booth across from ours. "Careful when you order. Spell it all out."

Mac was biting his bottom lip to keep from grinning. I found no humor in the situation at all. To be fair, Mac was in a difficult position. Sassy was dating his son Jeeves much to the shock of the entire population of Assjacket. The sweater bandit was a notorious man-eater, but seemed to have her sights set on poor Jeeves in a big bad way. Jeeves was besotted and apparently they'd been indulging in public displays of affection all over town.

"Here's the deal," I said in what I thought was a reasonable tone, if not a bit loud. "You can keep the sweater you've destroyed, but if I see you in another piece of my clothing I will zap you bald."

Sassy's brow wrinkled as she considered the gauntlet thrown down. She was very attached to her long blonde hair. I silently went through my last sentence and made sure there was nothing in there she could misconstrue as French.

"How about shoes?" she bargained.

"How about I deflate your double D's?"

"Triple," she corrected.

"Whatever. You'll be back in a training bra if you steal anymore of my shit," I stated not so calmly as sparks flew from my fingertips.

Mac graciously tamped out the small fire I'd started with my itchy, sparking fingers. He was good like that.

"That's kind of mean," Sassy pouted as she sat down next to me and put her head on my shoulder.

I bit my tongue to hold back the unflattering name that was on the tip of it. I felt bad now... Big-fat-hairy-buttholes, she was right. I *was* being mean. It was just stuff—stuff was replaceable and I had a ton of *stuff* thanks to my dad's obscene shopping habits. However, Sassy didn't even ask before she trashed my stuff. It would be a little easier to swallow if I gave her permission to wreak havoc on my apparel.

Great Goddess on high, was this what it felt like to be mature and caring? Shitshitshit. I wasn't liking it. I dropped my forehead to the table with a thud and blew out a long sigh.

"New deal," I mumbled in a barely audible voice. I didn't want too many people to hear I was getting soft. It was bad enough they thought I was nice. "If you ask and I say yes, you can borrow it. If I say no, I will smite your ass if you take it."

Sassy laughed happily and then eyed my new bag—zeroing like an animal does with prey.

"Don't even look at it," I growled as she quickly slid away in fear. "If you so much as touch my bag I will decapitate you with it."

"Is it a Birkin?" she whispered reverently.

"Yes. Yes it is," I said, giving her the stink eye. "And it's *mine*. You can barrow the Kate Spade."

"How about the Chanel?"

I wanted to scream no, but I was turning over a new and uncomfortable leaf. It sucked, but at the same time felt kind of good. "Only for formal occasions and you can't carry makeup in it. The lining is silk and I'll flush your head if you mess it up."

"Sounds fair," she said. "If it were me, I'd say punch your nose up into your forehead."

"Well, therein lies the difference between us," I told her, secretly wishing I'd come up with the nose forehead thing.

"There you go with the French again," she griped. "Anyhoo, I guess I'll return the suitcase full of clothes I swiped since we have a new arrangement. You're the absolute best friend I've ever had." She hugged me so tight I thought she popped my ribs.

"I'm the only friend you've ever had," I wheezed out as I shoved her off of me.

"That's true too," she said with a flip of her blonde hair as she walked off happily.

"Wasn't she supposed to take our order?" I asked Mac as I watched her flounce away.

"Probably better if she doesn't," Mac said as he smiled at me with *that* look on his face.

"Don't smile at me like *that*," I snapped. I didn't want or need his approval that I was becoming a nicer witch. I mean I liked it, but I hated it too. Goddess, I was a mess...

"Like what?" he asked as his smile grew wider.

"Like you're proud of me or some ridiculous shit like that," I snapped and stared at my hands.

"But what if I am?" he questioned.

"You can keep it to yourself," I informed him rudely. "I'm not dealing well with all this approval."

"So noted," he said as he unsuccessfully tried to frown. "How about I order for us up at the counter?"

"Will there be cheesecake involved in the order?" I asked relieved to change the subject to food.

"Yep, and a whole lot more," he promised.

Mac was a man of his word.

Another reason he should pick someone better than me.

CHAPTER 5

"I have a food baby," I groaned and patted my overly full tummy.

Mac had ordered for a small army and I'd unfortunately done the enormous amount of food justice. At one point the Shifters were taking bets on how much I could eat. My buddy, Simon the skunk won. He, his girlfriend, and I had eaten lunch together several times over the last few weeks, so he had the inside scoop on how much I could shove in my mouth.

Wanda and DeeDee were somewhat appalled at my eat-a-thon, but my squeals and moans of joy negated the sheer amount of food I'd eaten them out of. Jeeves had even come out from the kitchen to watch me eat three-fourths of the cheesecake.

"You done?" Mac asked politely. He tried unsuccessfully to hide his grin behind his hand as he scrubbed it over his jaw.

"Yep." I reclined on the bench of the booth and sighed happily. "You're a smart man feeding me like that. I couldn't have sex now if you paid me. Oh, and by the way, I've got the bill. I'd feel too guilty if you picked up the check. It has to be *huge*."

"Too bad," he said as he pulled my sloth-like body up from the bench. "Already taken care of. We're going on a motorcycle ride now."

"Fine," I grumbled. A nap would have been nicer. "Let me use the ladies' room and I'll meet you back here."

As I wandered to the back of the diner accepting congratulations on my eating prowess, I had a strange feeling. It wasn't a premonition and it didn't feel like danger. I wasn't psychic, but I could sense my obese cats somewhere in the vicinity...

What were my fat familiars doing at the diner and where exactly were they?

The ladies' room was next to the men's room which was next to a nondescript door marked private. However, *private* was spelled P-R-Y-V-E-T...

Interesting.

I was fairly sure I'd just discovered the secret lair of the gambling ring. My cats couldn't spell to save their enormous asses—bad grammar followed them everywhere.

Pressing my ear against the door, I grinned. They were so busted, but they weren't alone. Along with their gravely wise guy voices, I heard my dad. That wasn't a big surprise, but the conversation was heated and that was unusual. Fabio and the cats got along grandly—or so I'd thought. Eavesdropping was bad form, but they were talking about me. No one had ever accused me of good form and I certainly wasn't going to start today.

Zapping myself invisible would work for about ten minutes. Getting through a closed door undetected was a bit more difficult. Shit. Thankfully there was a hole above the door. The broken out vent would have to suffice. Damn good thing I was limber. A silent entrance was going to be a little tricky.

Making it through the vent quietly was the easy part. Listening to the discussion? Not so much. Why did doing things you shouldn't always bite you in the ass? Hard.

"She should be dating warlocks not animals," my dad hissed as he paced the floor and counted his wad of cash.

"Fabio," Fat Bastard said as he shuffled a deck of cards with expertise. "She don't like warlocks. They're all jackasses."

"Excuse me?" Fabio snapped and narrowed his eyes dangerously at the chubby feline.

"Present company excluded," Fat Bastard said with a smirk not meaning a word of it. "You should be happy she's dating at all."

"What does that mean?" Fabio asked with a snarl. "My little girl is perfect."

"Dude, dude, dude," Boba Fett said, "Zelda is definitely a hot piece of ass, but she's a little whack-a-doo."

"Do not *ever* refer to my daughter's ass or I will ensure you can't sit on yours for a century. And as far a whack-a-doo goes, she comes by it naturally. Her mother was certifiable."

Oh my Goddess, did *everyone* think I was nuts? I mean *I* knew I was crazy, but...

"Zelda's just fine the way she is," Jango Fett argued taking a break from tonguing his nads. "She has to find someone whose balls won't shrink up into his stomach and can handle all that hot witchy-booby wonderment. She's being groomed to be the... "

"Don't go there," Dad growled and took a seat at the card table.

"The booby part?" Jango, as usual, was confused.

What the hell were they talking about and what was I being groomed for?

Fabio didn't reply, much to my disappointment. He simply shot a look at Jango that made my cat slink under the table. As they all sat in silence, I considered dropping the invisibility and violently zapping the information I wanted out of the quartet. However, if I revealed myself I'd have a difficult time snooping in the future. What to do...

"Back to the original topic," Dad said on a long sigh. "I don't think I'm well liked in town."

"Ya think three-fourths of the good people of Assjacket owing you money might have something to do with that?" Fat Bastard offered cautiously.

"Possibly," Fabio surmised as he stared at the cash in front of him on the table. "I won fair and square."

The grunts of laughter were loud and Dad even joined in. Goddess, at this rate my newly acquired parental unit was going to get run out of town before I really got to know him like I wanted to. Crap.

"Wait!" Dad yelled as he scooped up the cash in his hands and waved it in the air. "The treasury is broke. What if I funded the musical and repaired the town's thespian reputation? They'd have to let me direct the show then."

"We have lesbians here?" Boba Fett asked, confused.

"Lesbians ain't no problem," Fat Bastard purred and grabbed his kitty privates. "A little girl- on-girl action is hot. I wouldn't mind seeing Zelda and Sassy do a little lesbian thing."

"I said *thespian*," Fabio corrected them with a disgusted eye roll. "And if you mention my daughter in a sexual way again I'll call in your debts to me and buy Zelda a dog."

"Harsh, dude. I thought maybe you'd developed a lisp," Boba explained with a shrug. "And what the hell is a thespian anyway?"

"It means actor, you imbecile. But they don't want me to direct their show," Fabio complained.

"Who don't want you?" Fat Bastard hissed as he extended his sharp claws. "The lesbians?"

"Do we need to kick some ass?" Jango demanded as little sparks of magic wafted around him.

"It's a bit tricky to kick a lesbian's ass," Fat Bastard informed the group of idiots.

"Sweet Goddess on high," my dad shouted. "Thespian *not* lesbian."

"My bad," Fat Bastard apologized clearly confused as to what he was sorry for.

"No ass kicking of the *thespians*," Fabio warned. "I don't want to win with magic or violence this time. I want to make real friends. I've never actually had real friends."

"We're your friends," Boba volunteered as he waddled over and patted my dad on the back.

"This is true and for that I am thankful," Fabio said with a smile as he slumped in his chair. "However, I'd like some human friends. I want to be part of something bigger than shopping or poker. Zelda's made me realize that I want a real life. I want to be a dad that she's proud of."

Human shuman," Fat Bastard grunted. "You're a great fucking dad. Everyone in this town would be lucky to have a friend like you. You're the finest card cheatin' mother humper I've ever had the honor of getting my sphincter handed to me by before."

"Damn straight," Jango agreed. "I say we just off whoever don't like you. The Bastard is outstanding at making things look like an accident."

Fat Bastard preened under the dubious praise.

"He's correct. You just give me the name of the lesbian that needs a shake down and I'll take care of it for you," Fat Bastard promised.

The silence in the room was palpable as they all stared at Fat Bastard in different variations of confusion and disgust. The obese cat was oblivious to the weighted silence as he went back to cleaning his no-nos.

"Again, I said *thespians*. Your political incorrectness is going to make you more unpopular than I am," Fabio said wearily. "I suppose I'll just have to give up on my dream of directing. I won't make Zelda do something she doesn't want to do. She's really warmed up to me and I can't risk losing that."

"You don't think she would go for it with Sassy?" Fat Bastard asked not even glancing up from his tiny balls.

The small explosion of magic that flew from my father's hands hurled Fat Bastard across the room and into the wall with a thud. Everyone—including me—quickly ducked to avoid the ricochet. Whenever one of the cats got nailed, the magic flew back in defense. Even invisible, I was certain I could get singed.

I knew my minutes of invisibility were numbered. I definitely had a few questions, but now was not the time for an interrogation. I had to pee like a racehorse and revealing myself would cause more problems than I wanted or had the time to deal with at the moment. Plus, getting them to come clean would only lead to more questions I was positive I didn't want the answers to…

Quietly climbing back out of the room, I walked away. I probably should have run, but my bladder and my curiosity had thwarted that plan.

Following my instincts had been second nature before I'd landed in Assjacket. Now I cared. Caring sucked. Liking people was complicated. Protecting my heart was always my motto up until a few weeks ago. Now it seemed to be growing and breaking into little pieces all the time.

Best thing to do when you don't know what to do?

Ignore it.

Pee.

Go on a motorcycle ride with a hot dude who won't have sex with you.

Win-win-win.

Maybe...

CHAPTER 6

"You're awfully quiet," Mac said as he pulled over to the side of the road and flicked off the ignition on the motorcycle.

He was correct. I had a lot on my mind. Mac was used to me shouting nonsense over the roar of his bike while we rode. Being a Shifter, his hearing was supersonic and he could always understand what I was babbling about. Today was different—so very different.

"I was thinking," I told him as I removed my helmet and hopped off the bike.

He pocketed the keys, put the kickstand down and then stared at me waiting for a diatribe to pour forth. Surprisingly nothing came out of my mouth.

"Thinking can be a dangerous hobby," he said as he took my hand and led me over to a dirt trail. "I say you just let it go for the afternoon and let me take you somewhere secret."

"Secret?" I asked, intrigued.

"Yup. Come with me."

I squeezed his hand and followed. Little did he know I would probably follow him straight to hell if he asked me to...

Colorful leaves still clung to the huge trees. There was a nip in the November air, but it was far warmer than usual. Sticks and fallen leaves crunched under our feet as we trekked to Mac's secret place. Normally I'd be making up a scenario that would lead to sex, but that was off limits and shockingly, I was okay with that. Not that I didn't want to do the deed with Mac—he was sex-on-a-stick personified—but maybe Roger was right. Maybe I'd missed a few things. Maybe if I got to really know Mac I wouldn't even like him... *yeah, right.* It was the exact opposite. If he really got to know me he'd run for the hills.

Was that what I was afraid of?

"Close your eyes," he instructed as we came to a clearing and stopped.

It was a huge grassy field with a pond in the center. The sunlight reflected off the water and made the late fall leaves shimmer. It was magical.

"But I already see it," I told him, taking in the gorgeous place.

"No," he corrected quietly. "You don't. Close your eyes, pretty girl."

"Is my tree house here?" I inquired and did as he requested.

"It might be," he replied with a chuckle.

We walked a few more feet and then halted. Mac gently pulled me to a seated position on the ground and then sat beside me. A light fragrant wind blew and I breathed in the air happily.

"Can I open my eyes?"

"Nope. I'm going to tell you a story."

"Like Rapunzel?" I asked with a huge grin.

His laugh made me shiver with delight. Had he changed his mind about climbing my hair and doing me till I couldn't walk? Goddess, I hoped so.

"Not like Rapunzel. It's a story about a little boy. You wanna hear it?"

"Does it end where we have sex?"

"Well... it could," he hedged.

Good enough for me. "Yes. I want to hear it."

I heard him inhale and exhale. His scent made me weak and my inclination was to scoot closer. Sometimes I just wanted to crawl inside him and stay. That couldn't be healthy. I made a mental note to share this alarming barnacle-like need with Roger at our next session.

"Once upon a time there was a child. He had two parents who loved him and a younger brother he liked to wrestle with and beat the hell out of occasionally. The little brother thought he would eventually be able to kick his older brother's ass, but he was sadly mistaken. The younger brother was a pain in the older brother's butt."

"Um, that's kind of a weird start to a story," I interrupted.

"You're right. I digressed a little bit. The brother thing isn't really important. Sorry."

"No biggie. Get to the part where we get to have sex," I told him.

"That's not part of the story. That's up to you," he said, tucking my wild locks behind my ear.

"Dude, no brainer. You don't even have to finish the story. I'm all in with the sex part. Can I open my eyes and wrestle you?"

"Not yet," Mac said with a laugh as he pulled me close to his side and played with my curls. "You have to hear some more. You might not want to have sex when you hear it all."

"You'd have to turn into a troll for me to not want to do the nasty with you," I promised.

"Definitely not a troll," he muttered with amusement and continued. "When the boy was small he used to come to this secret place and wish for things. He wanted to grow up to be a good man and he wanted to always be able to kick his brother's ass."

"Sounds reasonable," I commented.

"Yep. The Goddess heard his prayer and sent him a gift. She gave him strength, power and an affinity for the earth. She told him he had to practice diligently and one day he would be rewarded with a second half that would make his gift whole."

"Did this little boy practice?" I asked, knowing I wasn't hearing a fictitious tale.

"He did," Mac said. "But as much as he tried he couldn't get it quite right."

"Meaning?"

"His flowers came up roots first. His butterflies had horns. Instead of jumping gracefully, the fish in his pond tap-danced. A big fucking mess." Mac sighed and pulled me even closer. "However, lately things have been a bit different for the boy."

Did I want to hear this? Hell's bells, I did … and I didn't.

"Can the boy still kick his brother's ass?" I cut in, hoping to go back to a lighter part of the story and possibly stay there.

"Yes. Yes he can and he kicks his brother's ass every Tuesday. Occasionally it's been close, but the boy has come out victorious."

"How does your little brother feel about that?" I asked with a smirk.

"Who said this story was about me?" Mac demanded in mock horror.

"My apologies. I was mistaken. Please do go on," I replied as I bit back a giggle.

"So lately the boy has produced flowers with the buds up and the butterflies lost the horns but seemed to have grown fangs."

"And the fish?" I asked wondering if they'd started twerking...

"Ahh, the fish. They have toed the line so to speak, but the rain is an issue," he explained.

"The rain?"

"Yup. Every time a certain girl cries, it floods the secret place and the fields explode with indescribable beauty. Which has led the boy to believe she is the other half that would make him whole."

"Is that the only reason?" I whispered into his chest.

"Nope. The boy knew she was his from the moment he saw her."

"Don't you mean from the moment he yelled at her?" I countered and he laughed.

Our first encounter had been auspicious. I'd saved him from the evil honey badgers but accidently zapped the bejeezus out of his ass, knocking him unconscious. I dragged his huge, heavy, bleeding frame back to my place and locked him in a cage. This didn't go over well when he came to. I wasn't too happy either since he'd bled all over my Prada. However, I healed him, shouted back at him, stripped my clothes off—much to his shock and mine and then banged the living daylights out of him. And this was my very recent history.

"I beg to differ about the first moment part. It was in the grocery. Remember?" he asked as if he had to. It was burned into my brain.

"You're correct. I saw you in the grocery."

"Saw?" he challenged.

"Fine," I conceded with a snort. "I accidently-on purpose *might* have touched your butt."

"Grabbed would be more accurate," he shot back with a chuckle. "I knew then, but I thought you were human."

"Human?" I asked with surprise.

I supposed it was possible. I hadn't used my magic in the nine months I'd been in the pokey serving time for killing my cat who wasn't even remotely dead. My aura was probably a little wonky—but human?

"Yep, it was a bit of an issue."

"You were going to try to mate with a human?"

I *really* wanted to open my eyes. This was unbelievable. Magical beings could not mate with non-magicals.

"I was in deep discussion with the Goddess who was probably silently laughing her head off," he told me with his own laugh. "However, after you almost killed me, I was greatly relieved to find out you were a witch."

"I saved your life," I yelled, completely insulted. "You were about to bite it."

"No. I was winning. I would have killed all the honey badgers if I wasn't trying to protect you," he insisted. "You were quite the distraction."

"Thank you," I replied, still a little miffed that I was underappreciated for my honey badger popping skills. "I was looking really good that day."

"Yes. Yes, you were—as always. And even though I could lose my alpha werewolf man card for admitting this, I will say you were insanely powerful and did help. I couldn't have done it without you. Well, I could have, but not with you there."

"I think I actually followed that," I muttered as I put my hands over my eyes so I wouldn't cheat and open them. His acknowledgement of my hotness and the fact that I was a deadly, unstable force of nature removed him from the *I need to smite your ass category*—for the moment. "So why are we here?"

"Because I want you to see what it is that you being here has done to my secret place," he said simply. "Keep your eyes closed. Let me get in touch with the earth."

His body tensed and the rhythm of the earth changed. A new kind of magic I'd never felt filled the air. It was mind boggling and a bit unnerving. The wind became a soft melody and it bathed me like the sun on a perfect spring day. The chattering of birds and frogs filled the air and made me giggle. The splashing from the pond were the words that filled the music. I was dying to open my eyes, but I stayed blinded to whatever was happening around me.

"Are you ready?" he asked as he pulled me to my feet.

"Am I?" I asked, unsure if anyone could answer my question other than me.

"Open your eyes, Zelda. See what you've done to me."

Slowly I did and I was flabbergasted at what I saw. Beautiful was a paltry word to describe what was before me. Riotous color rendered me mute. Delicate flowering trees were surrounded by blooming shrubs, and vines in every shade of the rainbow shot up everywhere. Hundreds of fanged, day-glow butterflies flitted around my head as their wings gently brushed my cheeks.

Dropping to my knees, I tried to take in the sheer beauty around me, but it was too much. How could Mac possibly think I was responsible for this? I healed Shifter boo-boos, ate my own weight in cheesecake and conjured up treadmills.

The pond rippled as the purple and turquoise fish hopped in and out of the crystal clear water. Multi-hued birds flew wildly around and sang joyously. This had to be what the Next Adventure looked like. It was too otherworldly for Assjacket, West Virginia.

"Did we die?" I choked out as my eyes began to fill.

"Nope," Mac said as he guided me to a bench at the base of a tree. "We've just begun to live."

"I can't do stuff like this," I whispered. "You've made a mistake. I'm not capable of this kind of beauty."

"Neither am I," he said. "Not without you."

"Mac, there's just no way," I tied to explain but my tears blurred my words.

And then it happened.

And it was so simple, so wonderful and so terrifying.

As my tears fell from my eyes the rain fell from the sky. The sun didn't hide away, it grew stronger and brighter. The harder I cried the faster the rain fell. Rainbows shot out from behind the puffy white clouds and sparkled like glitter in the sky.

Mac took my hands and I felt a powerful magic flow between us. As breathtakingly gorgeous as the surroundings were, nothing was more beautiful than the man staring at me with so many unanswered questions in his eyes. Was it really true that together we were capable of making this kind of beauty? Could I trust this? Would I fuck it up?

"There's another surprise," Mac said as he tilted my chin up to the branches of the tree above our bench.

Sweet Goddess on bender, now I was certain I was going to turn Mac's secret place into a flood plain. In the strong and thick branches of the tree was a darling little house. The kind of tree house every little girl dreamt of. The windows had window boxes with peach and lemon yellow flowers spilling from them. Sheer curtains floated in the breeze and there was a porch with rockers on it. It was mesmerizing.

"For me?" I blubbered as I held on to him for dear life.

"For you," he said. "All of this is for you."

I was pretty sure what I was feeling was love, but I had a few things to do before I could say the words out loud.

"Mac, I... "

He quickly pulled me to his chest, making speech impossible. "No. It's still not time for decisions. You can't say anything until we've had all our dates."

His expression was worried and unsure and I hated myself for being the reason it was there, but he deserved all of me if I had it to give. There was only one way for me to find out.

I nodded and let my body relax against his as my gaze wandered over the Eden we were standing in. If this was really what we were capable of then I was going to work like hell to fix myself so I deserved it—and him.

"Take me to Roger," I said with a renewed determination to get my shit together. I was no longer going to protect myself in therapy. I was going to let it rip.

Goddess help us all.

Especially Roger.

CHAPTER 7

"You want to do *what?*" Roger croaked, paler and more alarmed than I'd ever seen him.

"Do you need the puke bucket?" I asked, concerned that the rabbit was going to lose his lunch.

Mac had dropped me off at Roger's office and I'd caught my therapist as he was leaving for the day. Of course it was after four so Roger's pallor might be due to drinking... Mac had no clue what I was so fired up about, but he was a very good sport and asked no questions. I'd like to think it was because he trusted my intuition, but more likely he was terrified.

"Just repeat what you just said so I'm sure I heard you correctly," Roger requested shakily.

"Okay, here's the deal," I began enthusiastically and placed the puke bucket at his feet as a precautionary measure. "I want to do two-a-day therapy sessions until I'm fixed—possibly three-a-day because I'm kind of in a time crunch here. I refuse to use my tree house until I can do so without guilt. And I *really* want to use my tree house."

"Tree house?" he queried cautiously.

"Yep, it's totally awesome and I'll have you there for lunch after I'm fixed up and functional."

"I see," he murmured as he jotted wildly on a notepad.

"Along with the massive quantities of head shrinking I'm going to do, I've decided to star in the play."

"My goodness, you have?" he questioned, very surprised.

"Yes. I'm doing it for my dad. He is not fitting in very well here due to his obsessive cheating habits and I want him to stay. Therefore, I'm willing to humiliate myself in front of the masses. I mean my Goddess, he was my freakin' *cat* for a few years. The very least I could do for him is give the town reason to make fun of me for the next decade or two."

"Is there anything else?" he asked.

"Yes," I stated with a wince as I sat down on the couch and put my head between my knees. "Do you have any paper bags I could breathe into after I say the next part? I'm afraid I might pass out."

"How about the puke bucket?" he suggested and held it up.

"Good idea," I said as Roger placed it next to me as I sat on his still ugly couch. "Mmmkay. I'm going to give Saaaaa... " I stuttered and got light headed.

I could do this. It was right and good and I was trying like a mother humper to change for the better—or at least a loose definition of *the better*.

"Are you all right, Zelda?" Roger asked.

"No. If I was all right I wouldn't be sitting here telling you I was going to give Sassy full access to my closet," I gasped out on one breath.

We both sat in frozen silence and waited for the world to explode.

"Shit balls on fire." I groaned and picked up the bucket just in case. "Did I actually say that aloud and we're still alive?"

"Yes. Yes you did and yes we are," Roger said with a weak smile. "Are you sure about all this?"

"Absolutely not," I told him truthfully. "Sassy will be taking her life into her own hands if she even touches my stuff, but she's a powerful witch. I figure she'll be fine with a few zaps and possibly no hair. I just think if I gave up some of my control with material things it would be okay for Mac to climb my hair and perform a private porno in my tree house."

"The same tree house you're going to invite me to lunch in?" Roger inquired with a scrunched nose.

"Um... yes."

"I'm going to pass," he said politely.

"I thought you were into porno, not that you'd be invited to that part," I quickly added.

"While I do enjoy the occasional adult film, I prefer not to know the actors," he replied primly with his hands folded neatly on his desk.

My grin split my face. Prim and porno didn't quite go together, but we were all strange—some more than others.

"Okey dokey then, we'll go to the diner."

"That would be lovely," he replied with a smirk.

"Back to the rest of the shit show I'm embarking on... the thought of doing the play gives me hives, but I'm fairly certain I love Fabio and I want him to be happy. Do you think that means I really love him? I mean I can't act my way out of a butthole, yet I'm willing to make a fool of myself."

While I waited for Roger's reply, I realized I was holding my breath.

"As to your question," he said slowly—so slowly I was starting to turn blue… "You are the only one that can answer that."

"You suck as a therapist," I shouted. "Here I am ready to lose my entire wardrobe to someone with knockers three times the size of mine and become the joke of the town by performing in a theatrical clusterfuck where people may die and you can't answer one freakin' question?"

"It wouldn't matter if I answered it or not," the bunny replied logically. "It would simply be my opinion. My opinion doesn't matter—yours does."

Son of a bitch, the rabbit was making sense. I didn't like it anymore than the *no sex* edict he'd shoved into my brain earlier, but I couldn't even argue with him. He was correct. I needed to make my own decisions. I just hoped a massive dose of therapy, saying goodbye to tens of thousands of dollars' worth of clothes and getting an ass load of heinous reviews on my acting abilities was going to be enough.

Damn it, it had to be. I wanted to get laid in a tree house.

"When is the first rehearsal?" I heard myself ask aloud.

Roger checked his watch and grinned. "In about fifteen minutes. Are you positive about this?"

"Nope. Let's go."

***

The Community Center was filled with Shifters who were so excited it made me queasy. My dad stood next to me, beaming like an idiot and accepting congratulations on his directorship like he'd just become the President of the Universe. I wavered between feeling good and nauseous— good because my dad was clearly overjoyed and nauseous because I was here at all. I was certain I'd made a very bad decision as I didn't even know what the hell the play was, but I was stuck now.

Even the grumpy members of the Town Council seemed happy with Fabio. It was most likely because he'd promised to foot the bill of the unknown theatrical nightmare with his ill-gotten fortune. It was win-win as far as everyone was concerned—everyone except me.

Bob the beaver Shifter stepped up onto the stage of the Center and clapped his small hands. My fingers itched to pluck his uni-brow that started just above his nose. I'd have to save that activity for another day. Bob probably wouldn't appreciate me sitting on him and removing an obscene amount of hair from his forehead in front of spectators.

Glancing around the now quiet room, my earlier confidence disappeared. All of my friends were here. Crap. I was going to have to perform in front of them during the rehearsal process. For some stupid reason, I'd had it in my head that it would be a one person show... maybe two. There had to be at least thirty Shifters packed into the room. Thankfully, Mac wasn't one of them. That would be a relationship killer for sure.

"I am excited so many of you showed up after the little mishap that happened last time we did a show. Your confidence humbles me," Bob told the group.

"Little mishap? People getting stabbed and eaten was a *little mishap*?" I mumbled under my breath only to be elbowed by my father.

Kurt the raccoon Shifter, Wanda's mate, politely raised his hand and waited to be called on.

"Kurt, you have a question?" Bob asked.

"Yes. Will there be violence or weapons in this show?" he asked with a small shudder.

"Um... no, not really," Bob volunteered.

"And what does *not really* mean?" my buddy Simon the skunk inquired with narrowed eyes. "I refuse to take part in anything with bloodshed, anyone losing an appendage or Goddess forbid, actually dying."

"That's a reasonable concern," Bob agreed somewhat nervously. "However, I am happy to announce the only weapons used in this year's production will be wire hangers."

A murmur of relief washed over the crowd, but I was fucking confused. Wire hangers? What kind of musical was this?

"What's the play?" I whispered to my Dad who seemed as confused as I was.

"No clue." He shrugged and pursed his lips.

"You agreed to direct and fund a play not knowing what the hell it was?" I demanded as quietly as I was capable of.

"You agreed to star in it with the same lack of information," he shot back.

"Point," I replied in fear for my life. "Can I get out of it?"

"Baby, you don't have to do anything you don't want to do."

He was sincere which made me feel like a slug. He wouldn't make me do this. I knew my dad would still love me even if I went running out of the door without looking back. And for that very reason I stayed. I'd have to discuss this one with Roger. It simply had to be love. If I didn't love my dad, why in the Goddess's name was I still here?

"I want to do it," I lied with what I hoped passed as a smile.

"No, you don't," he replied back with a chuckle.

"Fine," I muttered, totally busted. "I'd rather chew glass and swallow it, but I want to be with you."

Fabio's smile went straight to my heart and melted the hard shell just a bit. His eyes sparkled and he trapped me in a bear hug that I wanted to stay in for a very long time. However, his show of affection blocked out Bob's droning and I missed the announcement of the title of the show.

The applause was loud and the laughter was hearty. How bad could it be if everyone was so happy? Maybe it was *Grease*. I loved *Grease*. I would be an awesome Sandy or Rizzo. Actually I would suck as Sandy or Rizzo, but I did love the show. Maybe they would let me be the Principal. That was a small part and I don't recall her having to sing or dance.

"Sweet Goddess," Fabio shrieked so loudly I clapped my hands over my ears. "The costumes will be positively fabulous. Zelda, you will look like a million dollars!"

I grinned weakly and prayed he was exaggerating the cost, but one never knew with my dad.

"All right people," Bob shouted above the din. "Fabio will be directing, Simon will be musical directing and I will be choreographing along with having written the script. There are scripts and music available for everyone on the table in the back of the room. DeeDee will check them out to you. Not a word can be breathed about our production. The dumb-ass Shifters in the surrounding towns will try to steal our idea and beat us to the punch—especially the nosy chipmunk Shifters. We are gonna have a comeback with this baby and rule the you-know-what out of all the thespians in West Virginia!"

"Did you say the chipmunks are lesbians?" Jeeves asked perplexed.

"Um, no," Bob said. "As far as I know they're straight. I said thespians."

"Thank you. Just clarifying," Jeeves said.

"No worries. Are we ready to do a show?" Bob yelled gleefully.

The roar of the crowd was deafening and I still had no clue what the play was. How was this happening? And if I wasn't mistaken, Bob said he was choreographing. That didn't bode well at all.

"Are we starting tonight?" Sassy shouted from the crowd.

Oh my hell, of course she was here. I couldn't catch a break from her if it bit me in the ass. I wasn't strong enough to tell her she had carte blanche in my closet yet. That nugget would have to wait until tomorrow. This was enough for one evening.

"Yes!" Bob shouted back enthusiastically. "We'll start with the big production number, *No More Wire Hangers*. Everyone is in it!"

"Will there be sparkly costumes for this one?" a nice opossum Shifter named Annie called out.

"Tons of sequins," Fabio assured the happy group. "And probably marabou and go-go shorts."

"Awesome," Sassy squealed as she laid a big one on Jeeves who was clearly happy to be part of the debacle.

Of course I was still stuck on the fact that there was a number called *No More Wire Hangers*. Why did that sound vaguely familiar?

Oh shit. No, no, no, no, no, no.

This was not happening.

"All right Mommie Dearest," Bob yelled gleefully as he pointed at me with a huge grin that made his uni-brow drop even lower. "Get up on this stage and put yourself front and center! We're gonna swing some hangers."

No fucking way.

My body was rooted to the floor. Was everyone here smoking crack? Who in their right mind would think a musical of *Mommie Dearest* was a good plan? I suppose people that had participated in song and dance versions of

Silence of the Lambs and *Friday the 13*ᵗʰ were overjoyed to do anything that didn't include murder or fava beans, but...

On top of everything, the irony that I was about to play a mother from hell was not lost on me. At least I had *that* part of it covered.

Was I really going to do this?

Fabio was looking at me with such pride I almost cringed. I was certain he was mentally cataloguing my costumes in his head. His genuine elation was the only thing that made my heavy feet move. I wasn't going to disappoint him. I'd been through so much disappointment in my life I refused to add any to his. If this wasn't love, I had no clue what was...

I could do this for my dad.

I had to do this for my dad.

Shit. I was never going to live through this.

I silently wondered as I took my place on the stage if my monster-ass therapy schedule was going to go as badly as my decision to do the play. I knew opening my closet to Sassy the Booby One was going to land me in a straight jacket. The only thing that kept me going was the damn tree house.

However, I was beginning to wonder if sex in a tree house with Mac was worth the cost.

I pressed the bridge of my nose and inhaled deeply as Bob shoved a wire hanger into each of my hands. For a brief moment I considered strangling him with them, but I knew I would have to heal the little bastard.

New leaf, new leaf, new leaf. I was turning over a new leaf and if I couldn't hack it, I knew I could always run. I was good at that. I'd been leaving places my whole life. The only problem was I didn't want to leave this place. Assjacket, West Virginia was different. I was different.

I had made my plan of action and I was going to stick to it even if it destroyed me.

I observed Bob do something akin to a combination of square dancing *slash* twerking and I groaned aloud. This was going to be a long and painful rehearsal period.

Very, very, very long... and painful.

CHAPTER 8

"You say chipmunks are lesbians?" Fat Bastard asked as he searched the refrigerator for something that struck his fancy.

"What the hell?" I groused and slammed the fridge shut, narrowly missing his big, fat, square, furry head. "I said *thespians*. You have a very unhealthy obsession with lesbians."

"Pretty sure if we stopped using the term thespian altogether, there would be a far better chance of the Bastard not getting the crap beat out of him," Jango suggested as he wolfed down the last of the cookies from the jar.

If the cat hadn't offered up such outstanding advice I would have tackled him for inhaling the last cookie. However, he'd scored points. I hated the word thespian anyway.

"Outstanding idea," I said backing out of the kitchen just in case Jango went for the cheesecake. I wouldn't be able to stop myself from maiming him if he took the last bite.

I'd ordered six of Wanda's cheesecakes from the Assjacket Diner and we were down to only one. It was a draw between me and the cats as to who could eat more. Embarrassingly, I was winning.

"Anyhoo, rehearsal last night sucked," I said as they followed me to the den. "There's an awful dance number where we basically twerk with hangers."

"That sounds kinda hot," Boba said with a shrug and a kitty paw thumbs up. "You nekkid in it?"

"I don't know why I even try to talk to you idiots," I muttered wearily. "And no we're not naked, we're wearing go-go shorts and sequins. But the best part—and I say *best* with utter and unmistakable disgust—is me tearing around the stage screaming, '*No more wire hangers,*' while the cast twerks in terror."

Finally I'd rendered them mute. They didn't laugh. They didn't snicker. They didn't go for their balls. The cats simply stared in shock.

Damn. That didn't bode well. If my obese, profane, tasteless, whacked-out cats thought it was bad... It was really bad.

"You want me to kill the hairy beaver?" Fat Bastard asked. "I'll make it look like the untalented little son-of-a-bitch tripped because his brows messed with his vision."

Horrifically, I considered the offer for a moment. After I digested the fact that my cat suggested killing Bob while using the term hairy beaver, I quickly came to my senses.

"That's extremely nice of you, but no. We're not killing anyone because they're talent free. If we were, I'd be the first on the hit list."

"I call bullshit on that," Boba protested loudly. "You're a fuckin' star. I hear you sing in the shower. It cracked the glass on the fubashianass mirror."

"Okay, wait. Stop. What the hell does fubashianass mean?" I asked, blindly ignoring the fact that my appalling singing had cracked a mirror.

"He don't know," Jango snorted. "He makes up shit and tries to see what catches on. One place we was in, all the kids picked up on crapbasketasser. Them teenagers painted it on walls all over town."

"How'd that go over?" I asked, wondering if they'd been dropped on their heads as kittens.

"Got run out of that municipality with pitchforks," Fat Bastard informed me proudly.

The other two gave each other high fives and laughed like loons.

They'd definitely been dropped...

"Alrighty then, you brainiacs have to leave. Mac's coming over for lunch."

"No worries, Sweet Cheeks. We're gonna take some yogi with your dad," Jango said as he stretched and waddled toward the front door.

"Yoga, jackass," Boba corrected him as he dragged his fat carcass after him.

"No you're not," I said with narrowed eyes and my hands on my hips. They were lying sacks of shit.

"We most certainly are. I hear there's some lesbians there," Fat Bastard grunted as he got to his feet with a tremendous amount of difficulty due to his girth.

I closed my eyes and counted to ten. It wouldn't do any good to chastise or zap the politically incorrect dork. He was headed for an experience with pitchforks again and there was very little I could do about it.

"Have fun, make sure you cheat and bring home a few cheesecakes when you're done gambling in the back room at the Assjacket Diner," I said as I pushed them out of the door.

"Will do," Boba said with a salute.

"Shit, she busted us," Fat Bastard complained with a laugh.

"Told you she was smarter than she looks," Jango grumbled and swatted at his cohorts.

I shut the door with a little blast of magic, making sure it hit all three of them squarely in the butt. I'll show them I'm smarter than I look...

***

"Did you cook?" Mac asked with wide eyes and a horrified expression. He tried to mask his shock... unsuccessfully.

"I did," I lied through an innocent smile as I watched him squirm.

It was common knowledge that I was a terrible cook. Even the cats passed on my culinary attempts and they'd eat anything. Fabio had gamely tried to eat a meatloaf I'd created, but when he turned a scary shade of green I made him stop.

"Wow," he choked out. "That's just um... fantastic."

I let Mac freak out for two more minutes while I took the casserole out of the oven. This was fun. However, when I noticed him starting to sweat and glance at the door, I assuaged his fear.

"Of course I didn't cook," I told him with a huge grin as he heaved a somewhat insultingly audible sigh of relief. "I can't even eat my cooking. DeeDee dropped off a casserole this morning because she knew you were coming to lunch. I think she was afraid I'd accidentally poison the King of the Shifters."

"But then you'd have to heal me," Mac replied in a sexy low tone that made my knees knock. "Maybe a little mouth to mouth resuscitation."

"Hmmm, interesting. I could work with that. Maybe we could *pretend* I poisoned you. You fall down on the floor and writhe and moan and I strip you and heal you by riding you till you're blind."

Mac choked on his lemonade and grabbed onto the table for balance. He closed his eyes and started talking to the ceiling.

"What are you doing?" I asked as I piled the yummy smelling casserole onto two plates and added some crusty homemade bread DeeDee had thoughtfully provided.

"Praying to the Goddess for strength," he muttered as he sat down in the chair at the opposite end of the long table from me.

"How's it working?"

"If you stay four to six feet away from me it will work fine," he explained as he adjusted his jeans and quickly placed his napkin in his lap.

"Maybe all we have together is sex," I said watching for his reaction.

The thought was depressing, but what if it was true?

"I disagree," he growled, clearly unhappy that I'd even suggested such a thing. "Even though I'd give my left arm for you to ride me like a cowboy, I want way more than that from you. I want everything, heart, soul and body—preferably naked."

"I said blind, not a cowboy."

"Same thing," he replied, again readjusting himself.

"Nope," I argued. "If I were to ride you like a cowboy, I'd get naked except for boots and a Stetson. Blind means I'd just be totally naked. However, I'm wearing a fabu sheer mocha bra today so I might leave that on. So, cowboy—hat and boots. Blind—naked except for bra. Got it?"

Mac's head dropped to the table with a thud and the sound he made went right to my underused girly parts. I was being so mean, but he was such an easy target.

"I'm sorry," I told him and I meant it. "I'm not playing fair. How about I conjure up a long winter coat and one of those hats where just my eyes show? You should probably stop showering and maybe wear some preppy clothes like madras pants and a pink polo shirt. I hate madras pants—total turn off."

"Stop showering?" he asked with a pained chuckle.

He was jack-knifed forward and I was sure his Bon Jovi was killing him. My Little Red Riding Hood was making me squirm in my chair.

"Yep and wear preppy girly-man clothes, but that probably wouldn't even work," I admitted. I'd still want him even if he wore a clown suit, a man bun and black socks with sandals.

"Okay, how about this?" Mac proposed as he tried to find a comfortable position for his Bon Jovi. "All clothing stays put. We drop the poison scenario and go for the high school virgin and quarterback situation."

"Cheerleader," I added.

"What?"

"I'm a high school virgin cheerleader. I was never a cheerleader and I always wanted to be."

"Fine," he said as he stood gingerly and approached.

"Wait," I yelled making him stop dead in his tracks. "Did you bring condoms?"

"Condoms?" he repeated totally confused.

"Yesssss. Props are an important part of making it really work. Remember the Granny cap when we played Little Red Riding Hood? We *have* to have condoms. You have to show them to me and then swear on your life if I agree to do the nasty that I won't get pregnant."

"You're serious?"

He was torn trying to figure out if I was for real.

I was.

If I couldn't get laid, I needed the game to be realistic.

"Is your motorcycle out front?" I asked as I grabbed a jacket and my Birkin bag. "Wait, I might have some condoms."

"You have condoms?" he hissed through clenched teeth and a little bit of fang popping out.

Dang that was hot.

Shifters didn't use condoms. They couldn't carry disease and could only impregnate their mate after they were mated. He was clearly unhappy that I had any kind of sexual aid or block, so to speak, that might include someone other than him.

"They're not mine," I hissed. "They're my dad's."

The statement certainly brought the foreplay to an abrupt and very silent end—until we both groaned loudly in pain and started to laugh.

"That's pretty much a boner killer right there," Mac choked out with a shudder.

Shitballs, he was correct. I wasn't even horny anymore. The thought of my dad needing a condom was gag inducing. The thought of my dad needing a condom with Baba Yaga was scarring. It was worse than eating my cooking.

"I am so sorry," I apologized in a strangled whisper as I slapped my hand over my mouth so I wouldn't get ill. "Not my intention to kill your boner. I'm pretty sure my Little Red Riding Hood just locked the door and threw away the key."

Mac sat back down and grinned like an idiot as he tried to stop laughing. "Well, at least we know what kills the mood."

"This is true," I said as a grin pulled at my lips. "I suppose if we get out of hand we can just shout *Fabio's condoms.*"

"How about we shorten it to FC. I'm fairly certain if I use the term too frequently my balls will permanently retreat to my stomach," Mac begged in a brief respite from his laughter.

My grin now matched his and I couldn't hold back my giggles. Most guys would be mad that the amorous part of the afternoon was thwarted. This gorgeous man thought it was hilarious. Goddess, I was totally in lo…

No. Not yet. I wasn't fixed and functional enough for the tree house.

He deserved me at my best—or a good as I could get. And so did I.

"Do you wanna watch TV?" I asked, all of a sudden feeling shy. I hoped to hell he wasn't poking around my brain and hearing all my thoughts. It was one of his gifts— a most annoying one.

"I would love to watch TV with you. I also might be persuaded to massage your pretty feet," he replied as he stood and held out his hand.

"Can we watch *Project Runway*?" I asked as I took his hand and followed him to the den dragging the food with me.

He paused and winced just a tiny bit. "How about for every two episodes of *Project Runway*, I get one episode of *Deadliest Catch*?"

"I can live with that." I cuddled up to him on the couch and rested my head on his strong chest. He smelled so good and I felt so safe.

I found out Mac was very opinionated when it came to fashion. Much to my amused dismay, he yelled at the TV through all four episodes of Project Runway. However, his appreciation for Tim Gunn made his bad TV etiquette tolerable.

The foot massage was as close to an orgasm without having sex as I'd ever experienced and DeeDee's casserole was the bomb. The afternoon was perfect. He was perfect. The cuddling was perfect. It was just a damn great sex-free afternoon with a handsome, funny, smart man who laughed at my jokes and challenged me in ways I'd never known.

Now I just had to get perfect.

Well, maybe perfectly imperfect.

Hopefully that would be enough.

CHAPTER 9

Rehearsal was going *swimmingly...* that is, if you enjoyed drowning in hell.

"Um, Sassy," Fabio choked out as he partially covered his eyes. "What exactly are you doing?"

Sassy was playing my daughter Christina. While circling Jeeves, she was spastically and sexually humping the air around him. This was appalling and wrong on every level as Jeeves was playing Christopher—her brother.

"No, no, no! I did *not* write that," Bob the beaver insisted with a look of horror on his face. "She can't do that."

"I know," Fabio hissed under his breath. "I'm trying to let my actors have free rein at interpretation. It makes for happier thespians."

"Not working," I muttered as I watched Sassy continue her hump-walk. Thankfully she was wearing her own clothes. I'd hate to see an outfit of mine performing such a lewd move—I'd have to burn it.

"There are no lesbians in my play either," Bob snapped, wielding his script like a sword aimed at my dad.

"Everyone STOP!" Fabio yelled, bringing the rehearsal abruptly to a halt.

There were about ten of us in the Community Center waiting our turn to be directed by my dad who was incredibly close to zapping the hell out of his staff and cast.

"Let's get a few things straight here. The word thespian is now off limits. Forever. I am very open to your thoughts and character ideas. However, in the end, this is not a democracy. I see the big picture while you as actors only see your part. Sooooo, while humping the personal space of the man playing your brother is a *fascinating* choice, it will not be in the play." Fabio finished with a brief bow and put upon grunt.

Oh my Goddess. My dad was kind of brilliant.

"But it's an important and pertinent part of the story." Sassy slapped her hands on her hips to stop them from gyrating.

"How so?" my father asked gamely as he tried to hold his composure in check.

"Christina is adopted?" Sassy asked.

"Yes," Fabio replied warily.

"And Christopher is adopted?"

"Um… yes," Bob answered with wide eyes as he pulled on his uni-brow frantically.

"Were they adopted from the same mother and father?" she queried with raised brows and a triumphant expression on her idiotic, yet ridiculously attractive face.

No one wanted to answer the question because we all knew where she was headed. The silence was loaded. She was cray-cray and clearly over-sexed to have come up with this theory. Since no one was forthcoming with the reply she was waiting for, she unfortunately supplied it.

"It stands to reason since they're not blood related in any way whatsoever, they very possibly could have had a relationship. I say let's explore that and see what happens."

"Let me pose a question since I've been thinking about having Jeeves play one of the studio heads," Fabio ground out as diplomatically as a director on the edge could. "I believe Jeeves is not being used to his utmost ability as Christopher."

Jeeves grinned at the compliment and blushed sweetly. Sassy's eyes narrowed, but she was confused—as usual.

"Sassy dear, would you feel the need to swivel your hips if say, Bob was playing Christopher?" my dad asked.

Bob's gulp of fear made me giggle and watching Sassy seriously consider her answer was pure comedy—the kind that made you very uncomfortable and embarrassed for the comedian.

"I see what you're saying," she said with a serious nod. "I'm pretty sure I could hump anyone if it was for the good of the show."

Not exactly the reply my dad was going for.

"While I find your dedication humbling, I'm fairly sure I'm going to be ill," Fabio told her. "Bob will now be playing Christopher. You will not hump Bob. Are we clear?"

"Wait. What?" Bob screeched in a soprano pitch that put all the women in our cast to shame. "I'm the choreographer and the writer. I can't play a role."

"Yes you can," Fabio stated calmly as his fingers sparked ominously in opposition to his tone. "You will play Christopher so your play doesn't turn into a musical porno."

Bob slowly made his way to the stage as if he was walking to the guillotine—whimpering the entire way.

"Let's try a scene with Zelda," Fabio suggested as he waved his hands and created a brisk wind that blew Sassy, Bob and Jeeves right off the stage and into the audience.

"Just take it from page three and give it to me with feeling."

"I don't even know what that means," I groused as I opened my script. "There's no page three." I held up the pages filled with nonsensical dialogue to prove my point.

"Oh my Goddess," Bob screeched, ran up on stage and forced his script into my hands. "This one is correct. Use mine."

I nodded my thanks and opened to page three...

What. The. Ever-Loving. Hell?

"I can't say this."

"Yes you can." Dad encouraged me. "It's your first big entrance. You just walk to center and talk—loud. Your outfit will be so stunning most people won't even hear what you're saying. The applause will be huge."

"But still," I started, scanning the page and wondering whether to laugh or snap my fingers and burn the offending pages to a crisp.

"Just try it, baby," Dad begged. "Please?"

If Fabio hadn't said baby and please, I would have walked over to Bob and shoved the wad of paper up his beaver butt. If this was a sample of his writing, it was no wonder people got eaten and stabbed during the other productions.

"Everyone in the room place your cell phones on the stage at my feet," I instructed tightly. "I can't risk what I'm about to do ending up on YouTube. And if anyone so much as breathes loudly I will crunch your phone under my Prada combat boot. I will also make sure you grow several warts and possibly a hemorrhoid."

The phones literally flew to the stage. Once I was certain the impending clusterfuck would not be recorded for posterity, I prepared myself to plunge into hell.

"Whenever you're ready," Dad said.

Inhaling through my nose and blowing it slowly out of my mouth helped tamp down the need to blow up the building. I liked most of the people here and I'd be the one to have to heal all the burn victims. Not a good use of time or magic.

New leaf, new leaf, new leaf... I was doing this for Fabio. Fabio was my dad. Fabio had no friends because they all owed him money. He wanted to fit in. I could help make that happen... Shit. I was trying my damndest to be worthy of the tree house. So if pretending to be an insane mother from the under world was going to get me closer to my goal... so be it.

Loud. He said loud. I could do loud.

"It's a rap," Bob volunteered with misguided pride.

"I'm sorry, what?" I asked, sure I'd just heard incorrectly.

"You're lines are a rap and I'll beat box underneath them."

"That's a joke, right?" I asked through clenched teeth as I began to glow.

"Um... no?" Bob whispered as he successfully pulled the right side of his uni-brow clean off his head.

Well, there was one less thing I had to do. Now if I could just terrify him into ripping off the left side.

The beat boxing started quietly and then gained volume and speed. It was atrocious. He would have been cut from American Idol after two seconds. Where the hell was Simon Cowell when you needed him? The cast moved quickly away from Bob as he spit profusely while keeping the beat.

Was I really going to do this? The hopeful expression on my dad's face said I was. Shitshitshit.

Here goes nothing...

"My name is Joan. I'm a really cool cat.

I'm an actress and a mom without an inch of fat.

Wash my face with ice. Smear my wrinkles with goop.

I beat the dog's ass if he takes a poop.

Wear my hair in a band so it don't get greasy.

Get laid all the time, but I'm not easy.

My kiddies call them Uncle. I call them Joe.

Can't remember their names, but I'm no ho.

I'm the greatest actress to ever live.

But if you put your hand out, I'm not gonna give.

I hate wire hangers. If you use them beware.

I'll yank you outta bed and remove your hair.

I like my vodka and the casting couch.

Don't screw with Joan, cuz I'm no slouch.

Word."

The room was stunned to silence as was I. No one was breathing at all—smart people. The tree house was going to have to live on without me. There was no way on the Goddess's green earth I was going to repeat any of that crap in this lifetime. Maybe I could offer to turn myself into a cat and be my dad's familiar to make it up to him.

"Is this even historically accurate?" I shouted as I tossed the script in the air and burned it to ash with a flick of my fingers.

"Well, I might have taken a few liberties to make it all rhyme," Bob pathetically defended his dreck.

"Dude, were you drunk?" I asked in the same loud voice that scarred the inhabitants of the room with my rap. My hands were sparking and Bob was seconds away from losing the left side of his uni-brow—violently—along with all of the rest of the hair on his body and possibly an appendage.

"Um... no."

"Zelda has a point," Fabio cut in swiftly with his hands in his hair. He'd worked it into an interesting hair-do. It was standing straight up on his head. "I'm going to do a few re-writes tonight. And we'll get back to the actual script tomorrow. How's that sound?"

"A few?" I snapped.

"A lot," he promised.

"Great," Sassy yelled. "I just want everyone to know that I'm a method actress and I'll be conducting myself as such during the rehearsal process. Do you guys think it would be okay if Christina boinked a studio head?" she asked in all seriousness as she held tightly to Jeeves.

No one would even touch it.

"I think since Christina had dreams of being an actress herself, it would make complete sense for her to prostitute herself with a studio head," Jeeves told her lovingly.

"Goddess, you are so hot," Sassy squealed as she dragged Jeeves to the exit. "I'll be home later Mommie," she called over her shoulder to me as they breezed out of the Center.

Again the silence was heavy. Again I wanted to blow up the building, but Sassy had left, so it was moot.

"What exactly did she mean?" I demanded in a low tone reserved for wiping out bad guys as the rest of the cast sprinted out of the hall in terror.

"I think it means she's going to be your daughter until the show is over," Bob choked out as he too high tailed it out of the Center.

I stared daggers at my dad who had the decency to look chagrined.

"How about this?" he suggested carefully. "We go home and I make a double vat of chocolate chip cookie dough and vanilla milkshakes."

I'm pretty sure my silence unnerved him.

"And a batch of brownies and a dozen oatmeal scotchies?"

"Two dozen," I bargained. "And you have to burn the cookies."

"Deal," he said with relief. "Is the wolf coming over tonight?"

"The wolf has a name and no. Mac is on patrol. Apparently there are chipmunk Shifters in the area."

"That certainly doesn't bode well," Dad mumbled as he packed up his directing gear, which consisted of his script, photographs of Joan Crawford and a beret.

"You think they're trying to steal our *play*, for lack of a better word?" I asked as I piled the forgotten cell phones in a neat stack on the table in the back of the room.

"Goddess no. No one in their right mind would want this piece of crap."

"See?" I snapped. "I'm not crazy. It's horrible. Bob is talent free—even more than I am."

"I'll fix it or we'll just do *Grease*. I love that show."

I was my dad's daughter through and through. "Me too," I squealed. "Can I be the principal?"

"Yes, baby. If we dump *Mommie Dearest*, you can be the principal in *Grease*. Let's go stuff our faces."

It was the best idea I'd heard all evening. I took my dad's offered hand and went out into the night with him. Maybe it would all work out.

And then again, maybe not.

CHAPTER 10

"I'm going to bed." I groaned as I tried to stand. I was satiated to the point of coma.

Fabio had made good on his word and we'd both eaten our own weight in sweets. Magical metabolism was the greatest thing ever. I might feel like poop on a sharp stick at the moment, but give me an hour and I'd be able to eat again.

"Shall I ward the house so Sassy can't come home to her mommie?" Fabio asked with an evil little grin as he waved his hands and magically made all the dirty bowls and plates float to the sink.

"While the idea is tempting, I'd hate it if someone needed healing and couldn't get to me."

"You're dedicated to your job, my dear. Me thinks you might like it."

"Don't think. It's dangerous. Speaking of a job, I need to find one where I get paid. I can't keep mooching off of you," I said as I one upped my dad and sent the dirty dishes from the sink to the dishwasher with a wiggle of my nose.

"What are you talking about, Zelda?"

"I need to be able to pay my bills and stand on my own two feet. I've almost gone through my pitiful savings and while it's really nice that you're loaded and all, it's not my money. Since I'm not allowed to conjure up designer duds anymore and I'm turning over a painful and vomitous new leaf, I need to earn my way," I told him as he stared opened mouth at me.

"Darling there's a very generous stipend for being the Shifter Whisperer and your Aunt Hildy left you a considerable fortune along with her house. Not to mention I've put half of what I own in your name."

Now it was my turn to gape silently. This was too much. The stipend was nice, but the rest was uncomfortably mind-boggling.

"I have money?" I choked out in a whisper.

"Money would be an understatement," Fabio replied with a lopsided grin. "You, my princess, are set for many lifetimes."

"But it's not mine," I argued, torn between screaming for joy or firmly but begrudgingly declining my windfall. My fingers twitched to go online and start buying all the things I'd been bookmarking for months, but that was bad. Wasn't it?

"It most certainly is yours. A gift is a gift and you should accept it gracefully."

Mmmkay," I said doubtfully. "But what if I want to blow the whole amount on purses and shoes? I'm not sure I should be trusted with an ass-load of cash."

"I see where you're going," Fabio agreed and sat down to think. "How about I lock it up in a trust and you have to go through me to get to it."

"Like Britney Spears and her father?" I questioned, wondering if Fabio was anymore responsible than I was.

"Who's that?"

"A pop star who had several identity crises and shaved her head," I replied as I plopped down next to him.

"Are you planning on shaving your head?" His expression was alarmed and he gave me the raised eyebrow.

I considered screwing with him, but I was too full to do anything where I might laugh hard. The repercussions could be embarrassing and highly unlady-like.

"No. No, I'm not. I'm far too vain to do something like that."

"Thank Goddess," he muttered and let his eyebrow fall back to its normal home on his face. "Then sure. We're like this Britney and her father."

"Exactly how much money do I have?"

"Can you handle the truth?"

I considered carefully. So many of my questions led to answers I didn't want to know. However, I was one who opened presents early, rewrapped them and then feigned surprise when I reopened them.

"Nooooo, but now you have to tell me, Jack Nicholson. I probably can't *handle the truth*, but give it to me anyway."

"Several hundred billion," he mumbled.

"That is wrong on so many levels," I shouted, mentally counting how many Birkin bags I could potentially own and then slapping myself in the head for being so shallow. "How many people did you fleece to have that kind of money?"

"Zelda," he reprimanded sternly. "I've been alive for hundreds of years and I only fleeced assholes."

"Define asshole."

"Castro, Mussolini, the king of England," he informed me.

"England has a queen," I snapped.

"I'm old," he shot back. "Plus I invested and spread the wealth amongst the poor of those countries. I'm not heartless. I'm just an outstanding poker player."

"Poker cheater," I corrected him.

"That too," Fabio admitted with a long sigh and a small grin. "However, I've given it up. You're not the only one turning over a new leaf. I too am changing—I'm changing because of you."

"I'm not worth it," I muttered rudely, still not ready to stop being mad at him. Why I was angry with him for giving me so much, I wasn't quite sure—but I was.

"You are so worth it," he stated firmly. "And I've let it be known to the world that I am no longer gambling."

"How did the world take that?"

"Some better than others," he admitted with a wince. "I'm dedicating my life to the arts, being a father you can be proud of and to getting into Baba Yaga's pants."

"Okay, all of that was pretty awesome except for the last part. You've just tacked on at least twenty more years to my therapy schedule. Roger is going to be devastated."

"Zelda, we're living in an age where parents and children should be open with each other—bond like friends. I read this valuable information on an internet parenting website," Fabio explained in all seriousness.

Parents and computers equaled a mother-humpin' nightmare.

It was time to fight fire with fire.

"So you want to be open and honest with each other?" I asked glancing around to see if there was a stray cookie anywhere that I might have missed. I needed caloric fortification to get through bonding with my dad.

"Yes!" Fabio announced grandly. "I want to have a modern relationship with my daughter."

"You asked for it," I muttered as I snagged a few crumbs off the coffee table and popped them into my mouth. "I like to dress up like fairy tale characters and play out a warped version of the stories before I bang Mac's brains out. He built me a tree house and he's going to climb my hair and then do me until I can't walk. He has an enormous… "

"STOP," my dad shrieked as he began to glow and levitate. "The internet is a filthy liar. I shall find the bastards who wrote those barbaric parenting sites and smite their asses to hell. The truth does not set you free—it scars you for eternity. It's like acid being poured on my brain," he bellowed in abject horror. "This is the most awful experience I have ever had and I was alive when they were burning witches."

He was now hanging onto the chandelier as he hovered above and had turned a foreboding shade of green. I would have laughed if I wasn't worried he might hurl on me. I waved my hand and produced a large umbrella just in case.

"Are we done here?" I inquired casually.

"Yes," he choked out, near tears. "We are definitely done. If you need me, I'll be at the bar in town downing alcohol. I need to wash a few images out of my brain."

"Good luck with that," I told him sweetly as I quickly made my way out of the den and up the stairs. I'd kind of scarred myself in the process of horrifying my dad.

The day needed to end. I was going to close my eyes and dream about my wolf. I just prayed to the Goddess that my dad's green face wouldn't pop up and ruin my dreams.

Fabio was a total lady-boner killer.

CHAPTER 11

"If we don't wake her up, we can do the deed while she sleeps and then we don't actually have to talk to her or look her in the eye," an unfamiliar, high, squeaky male voice chattered while chomping violently on something.

"YeahIdontliketoseethefaceorhearthescreaming," another grunted in an equally feminine tone for what I was fairly sure was a man.

"I really don't enjoy killing people, especially humans," a third lamented as it too smacked on something.

Human? These idiots thought I was human and they were going to kill me? WTH? And what in the Goddess's name were they chewing on?

I lay in my darkened bedroom and considered my options. I could easily blow whomever they were to smithereens, but I wanted to know why they felt it was okay to come into my bedroom and off me. I should have let Fabio ward the damn house. I was not in the mood to pop anyone. It was messy and I was a healer, for the love of the Goddess. I was seriously tired of people wanting me dead—my mother's recent attempt on my life was enough to last me centuries. This was rude and unacceptable. I was at a totally good part in my sex dream of *The Little Mermaid*—starring me and Mac.

"Do we actually have to kill her? She's very pretty," the first one whispered.

Point for the intruder. He might not have to die—possibly a thorough maiming, but not six feet under.

"If we're gonna stop the play we have to kill her. She's the star."

"Howaboutwejustbreakherlegs?" the marble mouthed dolt suggested.

And then they all started talking at once. Loudly. And they were smacking on what I could only guess was gum. All I could hear was high-pitched bitching and gum popping.

Wait. One. Minute. They were going to murder me in my bed because I was playing Joan Crawford? I knew I was a bad actress, but I did not deserve to die for it. I was done with this shit. And I was quitting the damn play in the morning.

"Goddess on high, hear my call

I am so fucking tired of taking the fall

Take the rude little chompers and render them mute,

Tie them in knots and, um… wrap the bastards in jute"

Not my best, but it would do… I was freakin' tired.

With a wave of my hand the lights blasted on and the intruders blew wildly about the room. There were some terrified screams from my uninvited guests and the jig was up—kind of. In reality *they* were up. Up on my ceiling. Tied together in a pretzel looking arrangement and secured with rope. Their mouths were sealed shut, but their jaws still moved frantically. The Goddess had taken me literally on this one.

The eyes of the little trio of turds were bulging. I wasn't quite sure if the ropes were too tight or if that was the natural state of their face. It was highly unfortunate looking and I actually hoped it was the fault of the ropes. The three men were tiny in stature, dressed in matching red overalls and all had a shock of wiry brown hair that stuck straight up on their little heads. They didn't look like they could kill a flea, much less a witch with the power I possessed.

I was the proud owner of my magic, my departed Aunt Hildy's magic, and unfortunately my mother's dark magic. I was a bad combo of juju. A magical menace who been rudely awakened just when I was getting dream-laid. These boys had fucked with the wrong witch—pun very much intended.

"Who are you?" I demanded as I got out of my bed and realized I was buck-naked.

The bulging eyeballs were now positively grotesque. I wiggled my nose and dressed myself quickly. Uninvited gum chewing assbuckets did not get to see my goodies.

"If I have to repeat myself, you're going to start losing body parts," I explained as nicely as I could under the circumstances.

I had to give it to them. They tried. However, with their mouths sealed shut it was difficult. Interestingly, it didn't stop their jaws from working a mile a minute on the gum. They were a weird science experiment gone wrong. I was certain they were Shifters, but I wasn't sure of the species.

Clearly Fabio and my cats weren't home. The ruckus would have brought them to my room in a flash. That left me to assume they were tying one on together at the bar. I was on my own here.

With a loud and nasty stinging green zap of magic I released the hold on my would-be killers' mouths. Immediately I wished I hadn't. The gum thing was akin to nails on a chalkboard. And the voices—oh my Goddess, the high, shrill, tinny voices.

"Imsurewegotthewronghouse," Marble Mouth shrieked. "Yourenotevenalittlebithuman."

"Ya think?" I snapped, wondering what exactly I was going to do with them.

"We weren't really going to kill you. I mean, I think we're supposed to, but we're not actually good at that kind of thing," the one in the middle promised, chewing so rapidly I was sure the gum would come flying out of his mouth.

"Didn't sound like that about thirty-eight seconds ago," I stated calmly as I took a seat at my vanity and removed a bright orange wand I'd won at a carnival from the top drawer.

Witches didn't need wands. Some used them for show. I used them like chopsticks to secure my hair into fabulous up-dos. However, these little shits didn't need that piece of info. They quivered as I waved it around menacingly.

With their noses twitching, eyes bulging and the jaws working over time, I almost felt sorry for them. They were pathetic and the red overalls were a disaster. The pretzel formation they were twisted into made them resemble a floating freak show.

With an eye roll and a large sigh, I tried again. "Names?"

"Chip."

"Chad."

"Chunk."

The names answered my next question as well. They were chipmunk Shifters—the C names gave it away. I should have been able to call it from the nose twitching and the gum popping, but it had been a really long day.

"Alrighty then, little dudes. I take it you're here to off me, as if you have a chance in hell of doing that," I muttered with a shake of my head. "But before I turn you into warty, smelly toads, you're going to answer a few more questions."

"Icantswim," Chunk, formerly Marble Mouth, wailed.

"And this concerns me why?" I asked.

"BecauseifyouturnmeintoatoadIlldrown," he explained in between chews.

"Again," I repeated slowly, as if English was his second language. "Why should I care if you drown since your nefarious plan was to kill me?"

"I see your point," Chip volunteered politely.

"Thank you, Chip," I said. He was the one that thought I was pretty.

"Welcome, ma'am," he grunted between chomps.

"Drop the ma'am. I'm only thirty and I find it insulting. However, I find it more offensive that you thought I was human and that you could come into my bedroom and end my life. You feel me boys?" I asked as I flicked my fingers and set the end of my wand on fire for effect.

"YesIcanseehowthatmightnotappeal," Chunk said, nodding as vigorously as the ropes would allow.

"I have a few questions and it would bode well for your chances of surviving the night if you answer me," I said as I pointed the fiery stick in my hand at them. "Sound fair?"

"Yes," Chad, who'd been somewhat silently gnawing on his gum chimed in.

The others nodded in concurrence as they too worked on obliterating the sugary piece of rubber in their mouths.

"First off, do you all have to chew that gum?"

"Um, yes," Chip said as he blushed in embarrassment. "If we don't eat nuts or chew gum, we'll eat the insides of our mouth clean off. We're vegetarians so self-cannibalism is not a tempting concept."

"Okay, gross. Please keep chewing, but try a little harder to keep your mouths closed," I suggested, trying not to gag at this new piece of information.

"Do you have any nuts in the house?" Chad inquired.

Goddess, there were so many ways to answer that question. I decided to stick to plain and simple.

"No, but if you don't cooperate, I'll feed you each other's nuts."

Radio silence. Blessed and total silence. I suppose I'd shut the hell up if I were threatened with eating my friends' privates too.

"So now that we're clear on ramifications, how did you get here? The area is being patrolled by wolves. You dudes don't seem to be the sharpest tools in the shed and I'm curious how you weren't detected."

"We took the highway," Chip said as he glanced at his buddies and gulped.

"What highway? There's no highway in Assjacket. You clearly want to eat nuts," I threatened.

"He means the treetops," Chad cut in quickly, not taking any chance of losing his balls. "We come in high so our scent couldn't be tracked."

"Why?"

"Wehavetostoptheplay," Chunk said, a mile a minute.

"Why do you have to stop the play?"

"Because it's ruining everything. If the play goes on and it's successful, we die," Chip told me.

"Trust me, the play sucks enormous wads," I muttered, confused as to why the success of *Mommie*

Dearest had anything to do with them seeing another day. "You realize your story has holes in it. I can pop your little scroties off with a blink of my eye. Being vegetarians I would think you might be a little more forthcoming."

"We can't," Chad wailed with his little eyes squeezed shut. "We'll die for sure."

"So you'd rather eat Chunk's man nuggets?" I asked.

"IcanteatballsIcanteatballsIcanteatballs," Chunk cried out shaking like a leaf.

Damn it, I knew I wasn't going to make them eat each other's nuts. I was unbalanced, but I wasn't insane—or mean. These dumb asses were working for someone—someone who had a vendetta against the theatrical society of Assjacket. Why the hell anyone would be obsessed with horrific theatre was beyond me, but Shifters were crazy.

"So it's a thespian behind this?" I questioned.

"He's not a lesbian, Ber... " Chip said and then blanched a frightening shade of white as the others whimpered in real fear at the unintentional partial reveal of the mastermind's name.

Score one for the term thespian...

"Who's Ber?" I demanded.

Again with the radio silence. However, it was now coupled with terror like I'd never seen in my life. My need to protect them from Ber, whoever he was, came roaring to the surface. What the hell was wrong with me? Chip, Chad and Chunk had come to kill me, or at least break my legs, and I wanted to keep them safe? Dang it, the new leaf was making me soft.

"Are you going to answer me?" I asked in a low tone that made them quake even more.

"I will eat my own balls if I have to," Chad whispered.

"It's not actually your balls. It's your buddies' balls," I reminded him.

"I will eat Chip's balls. Chunk can eat my balls and Chip will eat Chunk's," he gagged out as the others nodded sadly.

What in the ever-loving hell? They would eat each other's nut sacks instead of talking?

"How in the Goddess's name can I help you if you won't tell me what is going on?" I shouted as sparks flew from my fingers.

"You want to help us?" Chip asked doubtfully.

It was a fine question and one I wasn't certain how to answer.

"I'm not sure. You're weird, you have bulgy eyes and the gum smacking is almost enough to make me want to zap you into the Next Adventure, but the fact that you would eat your friends' banana sacks willingly gives me pause."

"Because we're kind of pathetic and cute?" Chad supplied hopefully.

"Cute is pushing it. However, you nailed it with pathetic," I said as I blew out the tip of the wand and shoved it back in the drawer.

What was I going to do here? I needed to know what they were hiding, but I was well aware they were not going to talk. Any idiots that would ingest testicles were firm in their silence.

Shit.

And then it got even better.

"Mommie, I'm home," Sassy yelled as she clomped up the stairs of *my* house.

Of all the stupid fucking things I had to deal with, I now had to add Sassy to the equation? Wasn't it enough that I had gum-smacking terrified chipmunks on the ceiling?

No.

Wait.

Maybe Sassy's method acting was a random ass blessing in very deep disguise.

"Sassy, get in here right now," I shouted.

"My name is Christina."

"Whatever," I snapped. "Bring your delusional butt in here immediately."

"Goddess," she muttered as she entered my room. "You actually sound like my real mother."

I quickly sat on my hands and bit down hard on my bottom lip. Sassy was wearing my hot pink Prada combat boots and they didn't even go with her freakin' outfit, which thankfully wasn't mine. New leaf, new leaf, new fucking leaf.

I needed her assistance and magically singeing the hair off of her head or zapping a few Mount Rushmore sized zits onto her chin wasn't going to help. It would have been terribly satisfying in the moment, but I was trying to think more long term these days.

"Sassy, I have a little problem and I need your help," I said, lamenting the fact that I needed her at all.

"It's Christina."

"Okay. *Christina*," I ground out through clenched teeth. "I could use a hand here."

"Does it have anything to do with the contortionist act of weirdos hanging above?" she asked as she walked over and examined the Shifter pretzel on my ceiling.

"Yes. Yes it does. And while they may be weirdos, they're growing on me, so let's use the term odd."

"I can work with that. What would Mommie like me to do?" Sassy asked as she tilted her head and poked at the frightened trio.

Shitfire. Kill me now. Was I really going to play? Yes. Yes… unfortunately I was.

"Well, um… *Mommie* can't get the information she wants out of the little dorks. They came here to kill Mommie to stop the play apparently. Now while I understand that I have absolutely no talent, I find it absurd that I should die for something that petty," I explained without choking or breaking into hysterical laughter. Maybe I was a better actress than I thought. "Honestly, I'm pretty sure they wouldn't have followed through on the killing part, but they woke me from a really good dream."

"Sex dream?"

"Yep," I confirmed.

"Do you want Christina to kill them for you, Mommie?" she asked with wide eyes and a sweet smile as Chip, Chad and Chunk shrieked and whimpered in fear.

"Um, no. While I find it bizarrely and alarmingly nice in a revolting way that you'd offer Mommie such a lovely gift, I'd prefer you just dig around in their brains and find out who sent them and why they're really here. They won't tell me even with the threat of eating their own nuts."

"Hmmm," Sassy said as she sat down on my bed and pondered my request. "Chipmunks have really small brains. It's not going to be easy for Christina to extract information without possibly exploding their heads."

Sassy turned away from the hanging and now gasping Chad, Chip and Chunk and winked at me. She was going to be the death of me, but right now I loved her. Maybe the added incentive of exploding would get my new frenemies to talk.

"Guys?" I questioned. "How's that sound?"

"Badbadbad," Chunk blubbered.

"It's not exactly the way I want to go, but if it has to be… so be it," Chip said quietly.

"Great balls of magical fire," Sassy yelled and began to pet the trio of incompetent killers. "I won't blow you up. Some say it tickles when I go brain diving."

It was clear that my pseudo daughter felt sorry for the idiots, too.

"Sassy's right," I told them. "I don't know about the tickle part, but she's somewhat skilled at extracting the truth. If she pulls it out of your brains, then you didn't actually admit anything."

"It's Christina," she cut it.

"It's going to be Bald Girl any second now," I shot back.

"Got ya," she said with a thumbs up.

Chad, Chip and Chunk glanced at each other warily.

"I suppose that would be okay," Chip said slowly with a shudder. "But you could be putting yourself in grave danger by knowing too much."

"Danger is my middle name," I said with a smirk. "And I..."

"Is it really?" Sassy asked, surprised.

"Is what really?" I asked, exasperated.

"Is Danger really your middle name? I mean, it's kind of strange... Zelda Danger. I guess it works, but I figured it was something like Zelda Donna or Zelda Tina or Zelda Jowanna."

"It's Claire and if you say anything else I will give you a pig nose and buck teeth," I warned.

Sassy made the international zip the lip sign and closed her mouth.

"Everybody listen," I stated as I wiggled my fingers and lowered the pretzeled chipmunks to the floor. "This is how it's going to go down. Sassy, I mean *Christina,* is going to take you to the basement for a little fact finding. It's a nice basement and easy to clean if there are any bodily fluids emitted during the procedure. Plus I can fix up any booboos—short of death that Sassy might cause."

"You mean Christina," Chad reminded me politely much to the great satisfaction of Sassy the evil method actress.

"Yes, that's exactly what I meant," I ground out.

"Waitwaitwait," Chunk blustered in awe. "AreyoutheShifterWhisperer?"

"Wanker. I prefer Shifter Wanker, and yes I am."

The little dudes communicated silently for a moment and then bowed their heads to me.

"We are honored to be in your holy presence," Chip said solemnly. "We are very sorry for even considering breaking your legs or harming you in any way."

"Holy is taking it a bit far," Sassy snorted.

Technically I agreed with Sassy, but I was the only one allowed to say it.

"*Christina* I'd suggest you keep your petty jealousies to yourself or I'll be compelled to remove the feet that are illegally wearing my combat boots."

"Roger that," she replied with a grin and an eye roll.

Back to the matter at hand.

"*Christina*, are you on board with this plan?" I asked wanting to get a few hours of sleep before sun up.

"Yes, but like I said the gray matter is sparse in a chipmunk. This could take a day or two," Sassy said as she picked up the twisted ball of chipmunks and headed down the stairs.

"The faster the better," I said as I watched her gently take the little goobers away. "And don't hurt them."

"I won't Mommie," she called over her shoulder. "I promise."

My life could not get any stranger.

At least I hoped not.

CHAPTER 12

"They're in your *basement*?" Mac growled as he paced my kitchen in agitation.

I nodded and yawned. It was eight AM and I'd barely gotten any sleep. My house was full of people and all I wanted to do was curl up in a chair and take a quick nap. Of course I'd dressed with care to offset the baggage I was carrying under my eyes. I wore a wildly colorful Betsy Johnson fitted maxi dress with my pink combat boots that I'd stolen back from Sassy. Lookin' good and feeling crappy.

My dad, Roger, Fat Bastard, Jango Fett, Boba Fett and Jeeves sat at the kitchen table drinking coffee and eating the coffee cakes Fabio had very thoughtfully baked. I'd eaten an entire cake before everyone arrived so I was full for at least the next hour.

"You didn't detect the chipmunks?" Fabio snapped at Mac as his fingers sparked with displeasure. "They could have killed my daughter and it would have been your fault."

"Whoa," I shouted as Mac lunged at Fabio. "First off, I can defend myself. And Mac *did* know they were in the area. It's why he was patrolling with the Pack. The chipmunks took the highway," I explained as I separated the two hot heads.

"Ain't no highway in Assjacket," Fat Bastard informed everyone as he hid some cake in the silverware drawer for later.

"The treetops," Mac said, impressed. "I didn't think the chipmunks were smart enough to try something like that."

"They're not smart and they're lousy poker players. I'm sorry I lost my temper," Fabio told Mac as he removed the cake from drawer and smacked Fat Bastard in the head. "I'm a little hung over after my father-daughter bonding with Zelda last night."

"Apology accepted," Mac said as he scooped me up off my chair and settled me firmly on his lap. "I'd die before I let anything happen to Zelda."

"No one is going to die for me or anyone else," I snapped, avoiding the fact that Mac had just made a statement that no one had ever made about me in my life. It was as scary as it was sexy. "The chipmunks seem harmless and I'm sure there's someone else behind it. They were afraid to tell me so I sent Sassy to the basement with them to pick it out of their brains."

"Sweet Goddess in an outfit from Walmart," Fabio gasped out. "Is that safe?"

"For who?" Fat Bastard grunted as Jango Fett and Boba Fett joined him in laughter.

"I'm going down there to protect my woman," Jeeves announced. "Fabio, I'd like the recipe for this cake. It's outstanding. Did you use buttermilk?"

"Yes! How perceptive of you." My dad beamed. He was quite pleased that the finest chef he'd ever come across liked his cooking. "You should try my scones. To die for."

"I'd enjoy that," Jeeves said as he picked up the baby blue tux jacket that he'd paired with stonewashed jeans, flip flops and a wife beater.

His look was so wrong it was almost right.

"We'll join ya," Boba said as he grabbed the two remaining coffee cakes from the table and balanced them on his head as he waddled toward the basement. "Sassy works better with an audience."

"Tell me about it," Jeeves said with a huge grin and an enormous blush.

All movement in the room ceased and I was sure I heard a few covert gags. The food in my stomach roiled and it was all I could do to keep it down.

"Ahhh, Jeeves," Mac said as he pressed the bridge of his nose and amazingly held on to his composure. "Remember our discussion about TMI?"

"Yes, Dad. I do," Jeeves replied, clearly not following where Mac was going.

"That son, was TMI."

"Ohhhh, I got ya," Jeeves said with a second blush that eclipsed the first. "Sorry."

"No worries," I replied in a strangled whisper and then remembered a piece of the puzzle I'd forgotten to share. "Oh and the chipmunks mentioned something about Ber who's not a lesbian."

"Ber?" Fabio asked, puzzled. "I know of no Ber who's not a lesbian."

"You know a Ber that *is* a lesbian?" Roger inquired.

"No. Do you know Ber the lesbian?" Fabio questioned Roger.

"Wait the hell a minute," Jango grumbled with a shake of his furry head. "I thought Ber wasn't a lesbian."

"You know Ber?" Mac asked trying to follow the conversation thread that was quickly careening toward hell.

"Nope. I don't know no Ber," Jango said.

"Maybe this Ber *is* a lesbian and the chipmunks outed his ass and are now running for their lives," Fat Bastard suggested with a triumphant look on his face.

"How can a man be a lesbian?" Jeeves added, further perplexing all the male idiots in the room.

"Fine point," Fabio pondered aloud with an appreciative nod for Jeeves' intellect. "However, are we sure Ber the possible lesbian is a man at all?"

"And what would Ber being a lesbian have anything to do with the chipmunks trying to kill Zelda to stop the show from being performed?" Mac asked with a disgusted shake of his head.

"Do you think this is all because Zelda's a lesbian?" Fat Bastard offered up while scratching his balls.

"Zelda is not a lesbian," Mac informed the room with a shit-eating grin on his face, much to my dad's displeasure.

"My bad," Fat Bastard said. "Wishful thinking. Maybe Ber is a lesbian honey badger who's come to off Zelda since she popped the shit out of about a hundred of them and there are no more lesbian honey badgers."

"It's possible," Jango said thoughtfully. "But Ber can't be a honey badger lesbian if Zelda popped all the lesbian ones. You follow me?"

Thankfully that nugget of stupidity silenced all of them as they tried to piece the fucked up puzzle they'd created into something that made sense.

"Um, none of you should think—ever again. Your heads might explode and I can't fix that," I said in a voice dripping with sarcasm. "Ber is the mastermind and the lesbian part came out because I said thespian. I'm going with the assumption the Ber is a guy—a really bad guy if the little chipmunk dudes' reaction to the mention of his name was anything to go by."

"I'm fairly sure I made the term thespian illegal," Fabio reminded me. "It gets everyone in trouble."

"Especially Fat Bastard," Jango volunteered as he ducked a right hook from the Bastard.

"Let's say we let Ber the *not a lesbian* subject drop until we get Sassy's information," I suggested as I gently pushed the cats and Jeeves toward the door to the basement. "Boba, you will share those coffee cakes with Sassy and the chipmunks. Do you understand me?"

"I hear ya," he groused. "I don't like it, but I'll do it because I'm turnin' over a new leak too."

"Leaf," I corrected him.

"I am," he insisted.

"You're what?" Damn I really needed to go back to bed. These assbuckets were confusing me more than usual.

"I'm leafin' the damn kitchen and I promise to share the effing cakes," he huffed indignantly.

"Mmmkay," I said as I bit down on the inside of my cheek to keep from laughing at my cat. "Works for me."

The kitchen was clearing out and I was glad. I needed a nap more than I needed to breathe at the moment.

"Zelda, will you be at both of your sessions today?" Roger asked as he put on his coat and slipped a coffee cake Boba had missed into his man purse.

"I have three today," I reminded him as he blanched and then quickly covered it with a professional smile.

"Of course you do," he agreed with forced enthusiasm. "I look forward to them. I'll be at the office if anyone needs me," Roger called out as he tore out of the house.

My dad and Mac stared at me and waited for an explanation that was not coming.

"What?" I asked, busying myself with clearing the table. I could have used magic, but I needed something to do so I didn't have to explain my aggressive approach to therapy. Mostly because I wasn't sure I understood my aggressive approach.

"You're seeing Roger three times a day?" Fabio asked cautiously.

Mac just leaned back against the wall with his arms crossed over his broad chest and watched me as a small smile played at his lips. It made me want to kiss him— even with my dad standing in the room.

I had it really bad. No one should look as good as Mac did.

"Is something wrong with you?" Fabio asked still stuck on the fact that I was attending therapy like an addict.

"Is that a rhetorical question?" I snapped as I plopped my butt down on a chair and sighed dramatically.

The question was fair. It was odd what I was doing, but I was doing it for a reason. Everything, including not making the chipmunks eat their man junk, was because I was turning over a new leaf. I wasn't the only one I cared about anymore. Come to think of it, I hadn't really ever cared for myself. I was on my list of things to learn to love as well. However, there was a block and I couldn't put my finger on it.

I was pretty sure I loved Fabio. And I was terrified that I was in love with Mac. I just was unsure if I loved myself. I was trying. Three-a-days were going to either help me succeed or ensure Roger's early retirement.

"I'm just trying to figure stuff out," I said not making eye contact with either of the men in my life. "I don't want to talk about it. Okay?"

"I'm good with that," Mac said. He walked over to the china cabinet and removed yet another coffee cake that had been hidden by my fat cats and placed it in front of me with a fork and a grin.

The wolf knew me well.

"I won't mention it again," Fabio promised. "That is, unless you want to talk."

"Nope," I said with a mouthful.

"Ohhhhh," Fabio said as he ran his hands through his hair creating an alarming look. "Big news. The National Association of Shifter Thespians Yearly wants to review our show."

"I thought we weren't allowed to use the term thespian anymore," I said.

"Did you even hear what I just said?" my dad demanded in a tizzy, wringing his hands nervously. "This is huge. This could be my big break to directing on Broadway or off-off-off Broadway. Or at least somewhere in Kentucky."

"Yep. That's great. And what's even greater is that the acronym for them is NASTY. However, unless you rewrote the entire *nasty* piece of shit Bob penned, we're going to get panned and your career will be over before it starts," I told him as I offered Mac a large bite of my cake without stabbing him with a fork.

I really was maturing…

"Well," Fabio began in a bizarrely high pitch as he rocked back and forth like he was on a ship at sea.

I closed my eyes because he was making me dizzy and his tone made me a tiny bit nauseous.

"There is one little itty bitty possible problem," he said.

"And what would that be?" I asked through gritted teeth knowing the answer would suck.

"They're coming in two days to see the show."

"Um, that's not an itty bitty problem," I hissed in a pitch even higher than my dad had just used. My coffee cake now tasted like cardboard and I started to sweat. "That's a clusterfuck in the making. We've had one and a half rehearsals and we have no script. We have one questionable dance number where thirty people are twerking with hangers and Sassy is probably going to hump anything that moves on the stage. Not an itty bitty problem." I ended my rant in a shout that made both Mac and my dad wince.

"I rewrote it. We're keeping the Wire Hanger number because it's just on the very outer edge of being so bad it's good, but the show is a one act now. It's short and to the point. You'll be wonderful. No rapping," Fabio vowed.

My dad was now on his knees in front of me giving me the big eyes. It worked far better when he was a cat, but it still got me. Part of me wanted to embed my fork in his forehead, but I knew that was bad and not what the new and slightly improved Zelda would do. However, it was tempting.

"You're serious?" I pushed out of my chair and with a quick pat to my dad's head I paced the kitchen. In my distress, I found three more cakes that my obese cats had stowed away. Well at least I'd be able to eat myself into a stupor after I agreed to Fabio's new and horrendous plan.

"You can do it, baby," Mac said as he very kindly paced right along side me. "You're a terrific actress."

"When have you seen her act?" Fabio demanded and then screamed in panic. "NO. Do not tell me."

Mac glanced at me quizzically and I just shrugged innocently. He really didn't need to know that I'd traumatized my father with our fairy tale sex-capades. Just as Fabio didn't need to know that his condom use was a boner killer for Mac and me. Total honesty was complete bullshit.

"How exactly do you plan to make this disaster happen?" I asked as I picked at the coffee cake, tearing the masterpiece to shreds.

"Well, Bob is notifying everyone as we speak and we're going to do marathon rehearsals until show time," Fabio mumbled as he went to the fridge and yanked out the ingredients for chocolate chip cookie dough.

He was going to need a lot more than raw gooey sugar to make me do this.

"I have therapy. I have dates with a wolf. Sassy is dumpster diving in the chipmunks' brains. And someone named Ber wants me dead—I think. Houston, we have a problem here."

"No, Jack Swigert. We don't," Fabio shot back with a grin.

"I can't believe you knew the dude's name," I shouted and gave my dad a high five. "I didn't even remember his name. I would have said Tom Hanks."

"It should have been Kevin Bacon because he played Swigert, but Hanks said it in the movie," Mac added with a smirk, not to be outdone by my dad's knowledge of useless pop culture.

Mac got a high five, too, along with a covert butt grab. These were my kind of guys.

"However wonderful bonding over our love of Apollo 13 is, we really do have a problem," I stated firmly. "No way can we do a show in two days. Even I know this."

"We can and we will," Fabio insisted as he shoved a full bag of mini chocolate chips into my hands. "I'll record a voiceover of all the dialogue and the entire cast will act it out like a silent movie except for the Wire Hanger number. No one has to utter a word... thankfully. And Sassy's absence from rehearsal won't be a problem. She'll be far better without practicing. Having her otherwise disposed gives her less time to come up with obscene and questionably legal character ideas."

He did have a point.

"I don't have to speak?" I asked warily as I tore open the bag and inhaled half of it.

"Nope," Dad promised.

"Not one word?" There had to be a catch somewhere. There always was.

"Not one syllable. Witches Honor," he swore. "I love you and think you're amazing, but acting is really not your thing," he admitted sheepishly. "But looking beautiful and standing center stage under a spotlight in fabulous clothes is! So it's a win-win."

Again, he had a point.

"And you really think the NASTY people can help your career?" I asked, absolutely adoring the acronym.

"Bob says they are *very* important and influential in the theatre world. He's been trying to get them to review his shows for years," Fabio said reverently. "This is... "

"A possible clusterfuck if Ber the hypothetical lesbian shows up and tries to stop our play and off my untalented ass," I reminded my dad. "And I'd also take anything Bob says with a vat of salt."

"Speaking of Ber the sexually ambiguous bad guy, I'm going to triple the patrol. No one will get in or out of Assjacket without my knowledge," Mac said as he gave me a quick peck on the lips.

"Sorry about our dates," I told him as he moved toward the door.

Damn his ass was pretty in his jeans.

"Oh we'll have our dates," he promised with a sexy grin and a wink. "I'll meet you at the Center on your breaks and between your marathon therapy sessions. We can go out back and… "

"Hello," Fabio grumbled, throwing his hands in the air. "Her father is in the room."

"My bad," Mac said, not meaning it.

Mac strode across the room, took me in his arms and laid one on my lips that left me breathless while my dad hissed and huffed.

"Later," Mac whispered against my mouth as I grabbed onto the back of the couch for purchase.

And then he was gone.

Goddess, I hated it when he left.

"He's a pig," Fabio snapped as he gathered up all the coffee cakes and put them in the fridge.

"Nope. He's a wolf." I was still trying to find my equilibrium. "And a really good kisser."

Fabio's groan made me giggle, but his next announcement… not so much.

"Just so you know," he said with a sly grin. "Baba Yaga will be coming to the show and payback is a bitch."

Great. Something gag inducing to look forward to.

Exactly what I did not need. Or more accurately, what Roger didn't need. Even the thought of my dad playing tonsil hockey with Baba Yomamma added on the possible need for four-a-days.

Roger was going to crap.

CHAPTER 13

"I believe your mother is at the root of your issues," Roger said as we approached the end of our third hour together.

The rabbit had cried when I suggested we go four hours, so I let it slide.

"Well duh," I huffed with an eye roll. "I knew that. I'm waiting for you to tell me why."

"No can do," he replied.

"What the hell am I paying you for?" I demanded.

"You're paying me?" Roger asked, surprised.

"Well I assumed you were going to send me a bill."

"Oh my goodness, no. The town is paying for your therapy. It's one of the perks of being the Shifter Whisper. I saw Hildy on a regular basis when she was alive."

"Wanker. Shifter Wanker," I corrected him.

"Yes, of course. Wanker."

"Why does the town pay for the Wanker's therapy?" I asked as I tried to get comfortable on Roger's heinous office couch.

"Well, um… most Shifter Whiswankers are slightly… How should I put this?" he wondered aloud.

"Cray-cray?" I offered.

"Oh no, I wouldn't go that far," Roger said with a chuckle and a kind smile. "I have found most Wankers need a few more tune ups than most."

"That's certainly a diplomatic way to put it."

"Yes, well I'm good like that," he replied.

"Speaking of tune ups, do you mind if I take a crack at your couch?" I asked with itchy fingers.

The couch clashed so badly with my Betsy Johnson dress I was getting a headache. It had to go.

"Be my guest, dear," Roger replied as he took a few books off his over-crowded dusty shelf.

"Goddess on high with the best taste of them all,

Roger needs a new couch so please hear my somewhat unselfish call.

The plaid is just fugly and won't match my dress,

Please give the rabbit a sofa that's, um... not such a fucking mess."

With a grand wave of my hand the horrible plaid couch morphed into a lovely dark cream brocade goose down sofa with matching pillows and a snuggly coffee colored throw blanket. I heaved a huge sigh of relief that the Goddess didn't zap me in retribution for calling on her to satisfy my anal need for pretty things. It wasn't *just* for me. Roger's couch had to be at least fifty years old—everything in his office was antiquated. Of course I could have used some of my newly discovered money and bought him a sofa, but I was fairly sure there was no good shopping within a three hundred mile radius.

"My, that was an interesting spell," Roger commented as he seated himself on the couch next to me and bounced. "Does the Goddess mind the obscenities?"

"Nah." I shrugged with a cocky grin, quite pleased with myself. "I'm pretty sure the old gal is getting used to me. *Son of a bitch*," I screeched as a violent wind blew me off the couch and a bolt of vivid purple lightning connected with my ass.

As I rolled around the floor to put the butt-fire out, Roger had a mini panic attack.

"Was it the obscenities?" Roger squealed as he quickly tossed a glass of water on my smoldering backside.

"Um, nope," I whispered through a grunt of pain. "I think it was the *old* part. Sorry," I yelled to the heavens.

As awful as a zap of fiery hot magic to the ass was, at least I knew the Goddess cared enough to set me straight. I simply wished she had a method that caused less scarring. My spells were going to kill me if Ber the lesbian honey badger didn't get to me first.

"Would you like some ice?" Roger asked with concern, as I was still face planted on his rug.

"I'm good," I ground out as I stood and leaned against the wall. There would be no sitting for me today. "Look Roger, I know you think I'm unbalanced to be spending an enormous portion of my day with you, but I just want to know for sure that I can really love someone—or what love actually means. I'm so terrified that this is all a mirage and once everyone really knows me they won't like me anymore, much less love me. I even understand that what I'm saying isn't rational. I just... I just can't let it go."

I didn't care that my ass was still on fire. I plopped down on the couch next to my porno- loving therapist and let my head fall into my hands. Tears rolled in fat drops down my cheeks and tasted salty on my lips. For a brief moment I wondered if it was raining at Mac's secret place. I desperately wanted to believe that it might be, but I wasn't sure of anything anymore. Therapy wasn't working. Maybe I needed to cut my losses and leave until I could figure it all out on my own.

Running away would break my father's heart. I had no clue what it would do to Mac, but I couldn't commit to him like this. I was still broken. I might always be broken. The need to crawl out of my skin consumed me. Why couldn't anything be simple? Why couldn't I be a well-adjusted witch?

"Zelda, it's going to be… " Roger started.

"No. Stop. I know you mean well. You're really a good head shrinker, but I might be too damaged to fix. I'm starting to bore *myself* with my indecision. However, it's real and… "

"You need to forgive and forget to move on," Roger said quietly.

His statement resonated, but confused me even more.

"Who? Me? Her? I don't know what you mean," I yelled as the tears continued to fall. "Can you be more specific?"

Roger scooted closer, put his arms around me and hugged me tight. "You have all the answers in your heart and in your head. You simply need to slow down and listen. There's no right or wrong here. I don't have the magic pill or solution. You do."

"What if I don't?" I whispered raggedly as I sucked back my tears.

"At a certain point it becomes a choice, Zelda. We can put the past behind us or let it shape our future for eternity. Your mission is to figure it out."

"How do I know if I make the right choice? It's not just me I'm thinking about here." I ran my hands through my hair in frustration. Goddess, it was so much easier when I didn't care.

"Occasionally we never know and sometimes it's very clear," he said as he gently pulled my hands from my hair. "Life has no guarantees."

"That sucks," I mumbled as I laid my head on his little shoulder.

"Yes," he agreed. "But it's not boring."

"Roger, thank you for listening. I don't think I'll be back. You are an awesome bunny and the porno thing just adds to your wonderful weird. I promise to keep working on my mission, but you're correct. I have to do it myself."

I kissed him on the forehead and waved my hand in a circular motion around the office. I thanked him the only way I knew how. Everything in his office was now straightened, dust-free and updated. I even conjured up an enormous flat screen TV so he could watch his programs in between sessions. I stopped short at providing DVD's since I wasn't certain of his preferences and didn't want to go there.

"Zelda, are you sure?" he asked as he took my hands in his and squeezed.

"Nope, but it feels right," I told him with one last hug. "I've gotta get to rehearsal. You coming?"

"I'll be there in a bit," he promised.

As I turned to leave I saw him take in his new office with delight. It made me happy for a brief moment. Maybe the key was giving people stuff. I had a bunch of money that I didn't really need, but that would just be buying love and friendship. Somehow, I needed to know I was worthy of love by just loving other people.

Shit. This mission was harder than avenging Aunt Hildy and popping the shit out of honey badgers.

New leaf, new leaf, new leaf.

Goddess, please help me make the right choices.

Please.

CHAPTER 14

Avoiding Mac was difficult as he was at the Community Center on my every break. I pretended to be engrossed in my script, but it was abundantly clear he wasn't buying it. He stared at me from across the room with narrowed eyes and arms across his chest. I could literally feel his frustration. I knew he was trying to poke around in my brain so I mentally sang Bon Jovi's *Livin' on a Prayer* over and over. That had to be painful as I sang in the key of Z minor. He then quietly left the Center all fifteen times. It tore at my heart, but I was so unsure of myself and my own judgment, I was dizzy.

"We might do better with no rehearsal at all," Fabio muttered in a funk as he watched all of us try to mime to his pre-recorded voice over.

It was a comedy of errors and I was pretty sure that wasn't exactly what our illustrious director had envisioned. If one more person ran into me or stepped on my foot trying to follow the weird ramblings of my dad, I was going to blast a gaping hole in the stage with a covert wiggle of my nose. Seeing everyone fall into it would greatly improve my mood. It was bizarre to hear Fabio shrieking "No more wire hangers" in his best feminine voice. Bob, on the other hand was in seventh heaven.

"This is the best show we've ever done! NASTY is going to love it," he gushed as he gave my dad a congratulatory slap on the back. "The abstractness is so fucking confusing, it's brilliant."

"Really?" Fabio asked hopefully.

"Yes," Bob assured him. "However, I do think the characters should wear large name tags so we can tell who is who."

"Good idea," Simon called out from atop a ladder at the back of the room where he was controlling the spotlight. "That will be a tremendous help in knowing who to aim the light at."

"I'm on it," Wanda yelled, holding up a black marker and a stack of poster board.

"I do sign language," DeeDee offered up as she bound onto the stage. "How about I sign the whole show while everyone is running around doing odd gestures?"

I bit back my giggles at the thought and then groaned when my father rushed the stage in excitement.

"Yes!" he shouted, picking up DeeDee and swinging her around. "That's an outstanding idea. We're just like Broadway now. Wanda, will the diner be supplying snacks for the patrons?"

"You bet," she said with a grin. "Cookies, cup cakes and punch."

"Can we spike the punch?" Simon called out from his perch.

"Why do we need to spike the punch?" Bob asked perplexed as he arranged the plethora of props he'd bought from home. Why in the Goddess's name did Bob bring plungers?

"It's a good idea," Fabio mused aloud. "Joan was a drunk of sorts and it would make sense for the audience to experience the extravaganza through her eyes. It would also make everyone slightly more forgiving since we're under such a time constraint here."

"So we're gonna liquor 'em up to get them through the shitshow?" I inquired sarcastically, yet thinking it was actually a good idea. If we got them soused they wouldn't even remember being here.

"Yes, we are," Fabio announced with a sly grin. "It will be method acting taken to the extreme. It's inspired."

"Are we going to let them in on the secret?" I asked my dad pointedly.

"Definitely not," he said. "It will be a surprise."

It certainly would. Hopefully there would be no drunken riot. However, with Assjacket's Community Theatre record, that was anybody's call.

"Unbelievable! I can't believe you would rehearse without me. I've got second billing and a slew of great ideas to make the show sexier and edgier," Sassy shouted as she blew into the theatre with Jeeves and the chipmunks.

Chip, Chad and Chunk followed her happily chomping away on enormous wads of gum. Chad and Chip held her hands while Chunk rode piggyback.

WTF?

"I know you," Fabio hissed as he approached the trio. "You attended the poker galas."

"Galas?" I inquired with a laugh-grunt.

"It sounds better than the back room illegal gambling ring," Fabio said with a shrug and then turned back to the chipmunks. "You are tremendously bad poker players."

The chipmunks voiced their agreement and bowed to Fabio.

Weird.

"Everyone take a break," Fabio instructed the cast. "Get Mac, Fat Bastard, Jango and Boba. Let them know we have a meeting. Now."

"They're right outside," Simon said as he cut the electric to the spotlight and climbed down the ladder. "I'll let them know."

All of a sudden stuff seemed real again and not in a good way. I was so wrapped up in all my own angst, I'd forgotten I had a job and possibly a new death threat against me. I was a witch who was supposed to maintain the magical balance of my town and heal my people. It was time to get over myself and protect the Shifters who needed me.

"You have info?" I asked Sassy tersely.

Mac and the cats came barreling in and the chipmunks backed away in fear.

"They won't hurt you, little pookies," Sassy promised the gum-smacking rodents sweetly. "I'll protect you."

Mac's growl reverberated off the walls. Now everyone backed up in terror.

"You're going to protect the animals that threatened the life of my mate?" he ground out as his fangs dropped menacingly.

He was hot and scary—but mostly hot.

"Oh. My. Hell," Sassy griped and stomped her foot, blowing up the far left side of the stage. "Whoops. Sorry about that. Zelda is my best friend in the world. I'd kill the shit out of anything that would harm her. My pookies aren't killers. They're just stupid."

"Yepstupidasaboxofhair," Chunk chimed in a shaky voice.

"Stupid," Chip backed him up as Chad nodded vigorously in time with his chewing.

"Out with it," I demanded. "Who's Ber? Why does he want me dead and what does he have against *Mommie Dearest*?"

"And is Ber a lesbian who's been outed?" Fat Bastard asked as he sharpened his little kitty claws and gave the chipmunks the evil eye.

"Is this Ber douche-hole a man lesbian or a chick lesbian?" Jango asked very seriously as he wobbled over to the chipmunks and lifted his leg to relieve himself.

"No," I shouted. "No peeing on people. That is disgusting and smells horrible. Your manners are despicable."

"My bad," Jango grumbled, lowering his leg. "Just wanted to show them who was boss here."

"*I'm the boss here,*" Mac and I said at the same time.

I glanced over at him with wide eyes. Crap, I'd just tried to usurp the power of the King of the Shifters—very bad form. However, he just winked and gave me a wicked-sexy little grin.

"My mate and I are *co-bosses* here. Cats, zip it. Chipmunks swallow the gum or I'll remove your teeth. Sassy start talking," Mac instructed as he took his place next to me.

"Umm, Mac," I said as my nose wrinkled in distaste. "If they don't chomp the gum they'll basically eat their own faces. I say let them chew gum."

"Seriously?" he asked with a wince.

"Yup," Chunk volunteered. "Seen it happen twice."

"I really don't want to heal that," I whispered with a shudder.

That gave everyone pause. The visual was too much.

"Back to the matter at hand," I quickly insisted before I could clearly picture the ramifications of taking the chipmunks' gum. "Give me the skinny on Ber."

"Who in the Goddess's name is Ber?" Sassy asked bewildered. "No one named Ber came up in their tiny pea sized brains."

She turned on the trio as her hands lit up with sparks. Sassy was not pleased with her pookies. The chipmunks began to cry.

"You said you could pick the info out of our brains," Chad whimpered. "We didn't have to actually implicate anyone. Our lives are at stake—and someone else's life too."

"Speaking of lives at stake… explain the plan to kill Zelda," Mac ground out between clenched teeth, still not buying the innocence of the rodents.

"You little dudes are going to tell them," Sassy said with an eye roll. "I'm not sure I can relay that nugget of misguided brilliance correctly."

"YouseewelostallthemoneyweowedBertothemagicalki ngofpokernandBerisgoingtokillusifwedontpayhimbackand … " Chunk tried to explain.

"Stop," Mac bellowed. "I didn't follow a word of that gibberish. Someone else talks or chipmunks start dying."

"I was able to make out *magical king of poker*," Fabio announced proudly and then quickly backed off when Mac shot him a glare that would make most run for their lives.

"Well, you see… " Chip stepped forward and heaved an enormous shaky sigh. "We lost all the money we had in a poker game with the magical king of poker." He waved at my dad who waved back. "That's not a big deal, but it wasn't exactly our money to lose."

"It was Ber's money?" I asked.

"Um… yes, it was Ber's money," Chad whispered.

"Is Ber his real name?" I sat down on a chair, knowing I was in for a long one and immediately stood back up. My ass wasn't ready for solid contact yet.

"Part of it," Chip said, terrified. "If we could tell you his name, we would but he has our brother, Chutney."

"He didn't just say Chutney, did he?" Boba asked, with a snicker. "What kind of bullshit name is Chutney?"

As much as I concurred with my cat, it was rude. My father's name was Fabio, for the Goddess's sake, and the damn cat's name was *Boba Fett*...

"Shut it," I hissed at my fat, manner-less feline. "Go on," I encouraged the frightened chipmunks.

"If we say his name, he'll appear," Chad explained with huge eyes.

His jaw was working so fast I found myself grinding my teeth.

"What in the hell can do that?" I asked my dad.

"A genie or a warlock," Fabio guessed with a shrug. "Neither is good."

"Still lost here as to why the play had to be stopped and Zelda had to die," Mac cut in, getting to the point.

"Ifthemagicalkingofpokerquitsplayingpokerwerescrewed," Chunk babbled.

Mac blew out a long slow breath and let his head fall back on his broad shoulders. "Tell speed talker if he says anything else it will be the last thing he ever says."

"Chunk, he doesn't... " Chip started.

"Gotit," Chunk choked out.

"We need to win back the money so Ber doesn't kill us and our brother who he's holding hostage. But since the magical king of poker has left the gambling life behind to become a world famous director, we're sunk," Chip told us.

"Big holes in that story," I said as I grabbed one of Bob's plungers and held it up in the air. "It would probably be really easy to suck your brain out of your ear."

"They don't have much up there," Sassy reminded me.

"Easier to get it out then," I replied.

"This is true, but I think it would be less messy to have them eat their own nuts," she suggested.

"Don't talk," I warned her, wielding the plunger near her head. "I'm not going to suck out their brains or make them ingest each other's balls. I just want to know what the hell is going on here and what we're up against," I yelled. "Talk, chipmunks. *Now*."

"Sooooo we figured if we stopped the play, the holy poker player almighty king would give up directing and go back to gambling," Chip quickly explained.

"We could win our money back, pay Ber, save ourselves and our brother Chutney, and move to Antarctica," Chad added.

"So killing me was your idea, not Ber's?" I asked trying to get the convoluted story straight.

"Not exactly," Chip hedged as he now chewed on his lip as well as his gum. "Ber told us to destroy anything that was in the way of his money."

"So we took that to mean he meant to kill stuff, but we're vegetarians," Chad said as if that made it all crystal clear.

"You guys really aren't smart," I muttered as I placed the plunger back on the prop table. "No offense."

"None taken, oh holy Shifter Wanker," Chip replied kindly.

"So Ber isn't trying to kill Zelda or stop the play," Mac said summing it up while squinting and trying not to grin at my new title. "You imbeciles came up with the half-witted plan all by yourselves."

"That seems about right," Chad agreed with a polite nod.

"So I say we find this Ber fucker and open up a can of whoop ass on him and his lesbian butt," Fat Bastard said as he began to glow dangerously. "We get this Chumpy dude back and be done with the whole frackin' mess."

"It's Chutney," Jeeves chimed in, correcting him.

"That's what I said," Fat Bastard grunted as he heaved himself over to the prop table and grabbed two plungers.

"I'm in," Boba and Jango shouted.

"Nope," I said as I removed the plungers from the Bastard's paws and tossed them back onto the table. "This one can be solved without magic or violence. How much do you owe Ber?"

"Two hundred grand," Chad whispered in in distress smacking his gum so intensely I thought he might dislocate his jaw.

My dad was watching me closely, as was Mac.

"Is my money in the bank here?" I asked Fabio. "Wait. Do we even have a bank here?"

"It's in the Cayman Islands," my dad told me. "I can pop over and be back in a half hour... if that's what you want to do."

"It is," I told him, feeling really good about myself. However, there was still a lesson to be taught to the chipmunks. "I will pay what you owe in exchange for your brother, but you will stay here in Assjacket and work off your debt. How does that sound?"

"That sounds great," Sassy squealed. "I wanted to keep them anyway! Jeeves and I feel strongly about adopting since he was adopted and I will be a fantastic mother to rodents with limited brainpower. This is like a dream come true."

Mac's gasp of terror was only matched by my own.

"Jeeves," Mac wheezed as diplomatically as he could muster. "My house isn't big enough now that you're going to have a family."

"No worries, dad," Jeeves replied as he bounced in excitement. "Sassy and I had plans drawn up for an addition."

"While that's an interestingly appalling idea," Mac choked out. "I was thinking more along the lines of you getting your own place."

"Brilliant!" Jeeves shouted as Sassy and the chipmunks danced around the room in joy.

"How exactly are we supposed to find this Ber?" Fabio asked the question that hadn't occurred to any of us.

That stopped the reveling abruptly.

"Um, I guess when we're ready we can say his full name three times and he'll show up," Chad mumbled as he turned as white as a ghost.

Damn, this Ber sounded like a really bad dude. But the plan was as solid as it was going to get.

I just hoped it went as smoothly as I imagined.

Who the hell was I kidding?

Nothing I was involved in went smoothly.

However, as Roger stated earlier... it wasn't boring.

CHAPTER 15

As the cast reassembled for rehearsal and Fabio poofed off to the Cayman Islands to get the money, Mac took my arm and pulled me into a corner.

"If you run, I will come after you," he warned, watching me carefully. "And for future reference, *Livin' on a Prayer* is my favorite song."

"You're a glutton for punishment," I hissed as I tried to pull away even though I was exactly where I wanted to be. "I'm broken. I'm not good enough for you."

"I don't believe that's your decision to make," he replied calmly as he backed me up to the wall.

His body was hard and it was plastered against all my soft. My knees felt like jelly and I grabbed his arms so I didn't drop to the floor like a sack of potatoes. If I were him, I'd kick my ass to the curb. I was a ridiculous mass of contradictions who couldn't make up her mind. I knew I wanted to stay with him, but was it fair if I couldn't love him?

"I don't know what love means," I whispered brokenly. "I don't know if I love you."

He paused and I was sure I saw pain in his steady gaze. "Love isn't necessarily a choice, pretty girl. Love happens. I can love you enough for both of us until you figure out that you're worth it."

I was speechless and humbled. The wolf was crazier than I was.

"Mac," I began, but he silenced me with his lips.

It wasn't a sexual kiss. It wasn't demanding or hard. His full lips were gentle and sweet. He ran his tongue lightly over my bottom lip and it almost stopped my heart. All the things he had just said were in his kiss.

He was giving me a gift that I so wanted, but still wasn't sure I could accept. I closed my eyes ad kissed him back. His arms felt like home to me. Mac's low chuckle against my mouth touched my soul and I wanted to crawl inside him and stay. He was more beautiful on the inside than he was on the outside.

"You do love me, Zelda and I'll happily spend eternity making you believe it. You are good, kind, smart, compassionate, and you have an ass that makes me weep. I'm lucky to have you and you're lucky to have me."

He pressed his fingers to my mouth so I couldn't say anything stupid. Then he turned around and walked out.

I touched my lips and slid to the floor. It didn't matter that the cold hard ground made my ass hurt like a mother-humper. I was too stunned to care. Was love that damn easy? If it was, why didn't my mom love me? I loved her. Shit, maybe I still did.

***

"All right people, we're going to take it from the top," Fabio yelled as he cocked his beret jauntily to the left.

He'd returned from getting the money and now it was time to get the freak show in shape.

"Why is there a hole in the butt of your dress?" Sassy asked as she posed in the splits holding wire hangers over her head.

"I called the Goddess *old*," I muttered as I yanked on my dress to examine the damage. Had I been walking around with my ass hanging out all day and Sassy was the first one to point it out? Crap, maybe she really was my friend.

"You want me to fix it?" she asked as she grunted in pain and gingerly eased out of the splits.

"Can you?" I asked doubtfully.

"Of course I can." She rolled her eyes and tossed her hair. "I fixed all of your sweaters I stretched out due to my alluring bosom, I'm sure I can patch a butt hole," she said with an evil giggle at her unfortunate pun.

"That pun was really awful and please refrain from saying bosom ever again." An involuntary grin pulled at my lips.

"Will do. But the butt hole thing was awesome. Right?" she crowed and wiggled her fingers.

"Awesome," I mumbled as I bit back a laugh.

My dress tingled and sparked. I gasped at my stupidity for letting her have a go at anything that was literally on my body... but then it stopped as abruptly as it began.

Slowly and with great trepidation I looked over my shoulder. Much to my surprise it was fixed. Not only fixed—it was perfect.

"Oh my Goddess," I gasped. "I thought I was going to go up like a fire work. You're amazing. Thank you."

"You're welcome."

Her faced glowed and her expression was almost shy. Sassy wanted me to like her—and I did... sort of. She was all kinds of awful, but there was also something good. If I searched really, really, really hard, I could find it.

Maybe I hadn't been looking hard enough.

"Um, Sassy... I want to give you carte blanche of my closet," I blurted out in a rush before I could change my mind. "You can borrow whatever you want except for the Birkin bag and underwear."

"Is this because I repaired your butt hole?" she asked with a silly grin.

"No, but my butt hole thanks you. I decided this the other day, but every time I thought about telling you, it got wedged in my throat," I confessed.

"It would have given me gas," she admitted me as she slowly slid back into the splits.

"However, I am wildly grateful and will repair any damage I cause. Can I touch the Birkin bag?" she queried wishfully.

I had to think about that. It was a difficult decision. I was turning over a new leaf, but that didn't mean there was going to be some leftover materialism. A girl could only change so much.

"You can sniff it," I bargained. "And possibly sit next to it, but only if I'm there."

"Sounds fair." Sassy smiled and blew me a kiss.

"While all this bonding is nice, albeit a little disconcertingly nauseating, this does not mean I'll stop giving you shit or threatening to zap you bald," I stated firmly, trying to keep a small semblance of who I was intact. At this rate I wasn't going to recognize myself next time I looked in the mirror.

"I'd expect and want no less," she assured me. "And I will continue to annoy the living Goddess out of you and behave inappropriately."

"This could work," I muttered aloud as I moved away and got ready for my heinous entrance. Any more bonding might give me hives.

"Zelda are you ready?" Dad called out.

"No, but I'm gonna do it anyway," I yelled back as I took a deep breath and said a quick prayer to the Goddess for the ability not to blow anything or anyone up during the play practice.

"That's my girl," my dad said proudly.

I was.

I was his girl... and it felt nice.

CHAPTER 16

"Oh my Goddess, I'm so nervous," Sassy squealed at decibels that would attract stray dogs within a hundred miles.

I glanced around the makeshift dressing room in the Community Center and grinned. We were really going to do this. DeeDee and Wanda had on more make-up than any drag queen would comfortably wear and were still applying. Wanda's adorable four-year-old son Bo was running around the room kissing everyone for luck. There was an enormous array of gorgeous flowers for me from Mac. The card was simple, but to the point.

I picked them from our secret place. The blooms are nowhere as beautiful as you. I'll meet you in the tree house after the show.

xoxo Mac

He was being awfully bossy, but then again I secretly liked that macho, alpha wolf quality. However, the tree house meant sex and sex meant mating. Mating meant embedded fangs in my neck. But mostly it meant I needed to make a decision.

I pushed the thoughts away and concentrated on becoming *Mommie*. I was as nervous as Sassy. I was simply trying not to let it show.

"Most of the audience is soused," Wanda informed us with pride and a huge smirk. "I made my Long Island ice tea. It's a killer."

"Are the NASTY people here?" DeeDee asked while dramatically signing everything she was saying to warm up for her debut.

I was pretty sure there were no deaf people in the audience, but DeeDee was so wound up I wasn't going to burst her bubble.

"Yep and they're wasted. Fabio has been plying them with drinks for the better part of an hour and I'm pretty sure Bob is puking his guts out in the men's room," Wanda said as she passed Bo off to her raccoon Shifter husband Kurt so they could get seated.

She gave them a quick kiss and let the male half of the cast know we were dressed and it was safe to join us. My dad had outdone himself on the costumes. They were so authentic it was almost creepy.

"How do I look, Mommie?" Sassy asked as she twirled around in a pale pink dress layered with yards and yards of frothy tulle.

"You look just like Christina," I told her, giving up my snarky ways and playing along with her game.

"Well, I should think so. Fabio procured all of the costumes from the private vault of Joan Crawford," she informed me.

"He did what?" I yelled and looked down at my mint green fitted silk shantung suit and gagged a little. Almost creepy was incorrect—it was truly creepy. "Joan Crawford wore this?"

"She did," Wanda confirmed. "I'm fairly sure Fabio procured the costumes *creatively* so everyone be careful not to ruin them. I'd hate to see our director spend time in the pokey for wanting us to look fabulous."

"He's never going to go on the straight and narrow, is he?" I mumbled as I took in the array of costumes with a critical eye.

"Oh heavens no." Wanda chuckled and shook her head. "You're father is special—one of a kind. He might have quit gambling, but he needs some felonious excitement. As long as he's not hurting anyone, I say fine."

"Could this generous description of my dad be because you look like a million bucks in your outfit?" I surmised with a raised brow.

"Possibly," Wanda agreed with a giggle. "Or maybe it's the fact that I had to sample all the pitchers of Long Island ice tea... "

Awesome. Wanda was tipsy and I was wearing a mean dead movie star's clothes.

I'd be having a chat with my dad after the show. We had enough funds to *procure* what we needed legally. However, I would not judge. Hell, it was all I could do not to poof to Paris and go on a shopping spree that would set me back a few decades. One day at a time was my new motto.

"Baba Yoskankaroo is here," Sassy informed me as she stuffed her bra with wads of toilet paper.

"What are you doing?" I gaped at her in shock. Her knockers were huge. She didn't need any added help.

"I want to be noticed," she replied logically.

"And falling over because your boobs are going to outweigh the entire rest of your body is your idea of standing out?"

"You might have a point," Sassy mused as she removed a roll or three from her bra. "Did you hear me? Baba Yobergermeister is in the audience with her icky little warlock posse."

"Heard and ignoring," I answered as I carefully applied blood red Chanel lipstick. Thankfully it was mine and it was new. The thought of wearing Joan's actual lipstick was gag- inducing and I wouldn't have put it past my dad to have *procured* that stuff too. "Baba Yoharshpunishment is dating my dad."

"Sweet Glenda the Good Witch with a broom up her ass, you're screwing with me," Sassy shrieked much to the distress of my left eardrum. "Baba Youmpaloompa is gonna be your step-mom?"

"If you value your life, you will never utter the words Baba and mom in the same sentence again," I snapped. "I already have one scary mother. I don't need another."

"Dude, sorry. I feel you on the mom thing. Mine left me at an orphanage for wayward witches when I was seven," Sassy said and then dropped her gaze from mine.

"For how long?" I asked wishing my mom had done the same. My childhood would have been a lot better.

"Um… for always," she replied and then went back to stuffing her bra.

Hell's bells, why didn't I know that?

Well, maybe because Sassy and I had never really talked about anything with substance even though we'd spent nine months in the magical pokey together.

Her lack of education and constant need for attention made a little more sense now. She was still a pain in the ass, but there was an explanation.

"What about your dad?"

"No clue who the sperm donor might be," she said with a careless shrug. "I've thought about trying to find him, but I'm sick of being disappointed. I'm happy here. I like Assjacket. Jeeves is the first man I've ever met that loves me for me. Plus he's hung like a horse."

"Didn't want to know that." I groaned and grabbed her hands before she could make her knockers so obscene they would be the star of the show. "Take the toilet paper out. You don't need it. You are fine just being you."

"Are you fine being you?" she asked turning the tables and putting an ironically pertinent question on the table.

After a long pause and an even longer sigh, I answered. "I'm trying. I'm really trying."

***

The Community Center was packed and my stomach churned painfully. Why in the ever-loving hell did I agree to this? I couldn't act my way out of a hole. Even though I didn't have to speak a word, I still had to pretend. This was not going to end well.

New leaf, new leaf, new motherfucking leaf.

"Okay everyone," Fabio whispered, more excited than I'd ever seen him. "Most of the house is blotto, so they're gonna love it. Just listen to the voice-over and do like we did in rehearsal. You will all be brilliant."

"What if we forget what we did in rehearsal?" Jeeves asked, slightly less bouncy than normal—and far more pale.

"Go with your gut and make it up on the spot. Just don't knock anyone off the stage," my dad advised. "All right everyone, take each other's hands."

Sassy grabbed one of my hands and my buddy Simon the skunk grabbed the other. I knew my palms were sweaty and my body trembled.

"You're gonna be wonderful," Simon whispered as he gently squeezed my hand. "I'll keep the spotlight on you and you'll be so blinded you won't see anyone in the audience."

"Promise?" I asked. Simon was a true friend.

"On my life," he vowed. "Just smile and look pretty. It will be over in fifty one minutes and twenty seven seconds."

My dad cleared his throat dramatically, wiped a fictitious tear from his eye and straightened his beret.

"Oh Great Goddess," he began reverently. "Please be with us tonight as we pull one over on our inebriated guests. We are the lucky ones to have been given the gift to perform *Mommie Dearest*. How blessed are we to be wearing the actual clothing of some dead and awful people?"

"Very blessed," Bob yelled as he entered the room looking like he'd been on a three-day bender.

"Just remember my friends," Fabio said. "When words simply aren't enough to tell the story, we sing. And when raising our voices in song can't convey our deepest emotions... we dance. That is the beauty of theatre. Our bodies are our tools and nothing can stop us!"

"Lack of talent can," I mumbled.

"Nope," my dad disagreed. "Lack of talent is a myth. All you have to do is want to be out there and share the four and a half hours of hard work we did and you will be welcomed with open arms and drunken love."

"Amen," Bob shouted over his shoulder as he ran back to the men's room.

Looking around the circle, I grew calmer.

Roger, Simon, Wanda, DeeDee, Sassy, Jeeves and the chipmunks were ready to go, along with many of my other Shifter friends. Chad, Chip and Chunk had joined the cast and were playing acrobatic B-actors that performed in Joan's films. Their excitement was palpable. They were fitting into Assjacket splendidly.

It was getting easier to ignore the gum thing too— well, kind of.

"Alrighty people, let's go!" Fabio saluted us and made his way out into the back of the house to run the sound. Simon followed to man the spotlight and we all got into our places back stage.

And the shitshow began...

CHAPTER 17

"Mother*fucker*! I think I lost part of my boob out there when I did the forward roll," Sassy lamented as we stood in the wings and watched the chipmunks make a lopsided pyramid much to the delight of the crowd.

Sassy was correct. There was a large wad of toilet paper center stage.

"I told you to take that crap out of your bra," I whispered as I waited in terror for my entrance.

The show was a hot mess, but the audience was loving it. Maybe Fabio was right. Just going out there and letting it rip would be fun.

"I got busy giving Jeeves a good luck hand job and forgot to take it all out," she replied in a tizzy. "Should I zap it off the stage?"

"Goddess, no. You might catch the chipmunks on fire and cause a stampede to the exit. We need to have a show on record where no one gets maimed. Leave it. We can pick it up during our scene," I told her as I tried to stop my lips from quivering in nervousness and block out the fact that Sassy had just told me she'd serviced Jeeves before the show.

"Good thinking." She quickly removed another huge wad from her bra and tossed it on the prop table. "Do you know what the plungers are for?"

"No and I don't want to," I told her as I bent over and touched my toes.

"What are you doing?"

"I don't know," I snapped. "I've seen it on *Dancing With The Stars*. I figure this is what you do before you go out on stage."

"Right," Sassy agreed and touched her own toes. "Um, Zelda?"

"What?" I asked as I stood back up and grabbed onto the wall so I didn't fall from the head rush I'd just given myself.

"You're on."

Shit. She was right. I was supposed to go out there and listen to my dad's voice and mime the crap out of what he was saying.

Was I going to really going to do this?

Sassy gave me a smile, a hug and a hearty shove.

Yep, I was going to do it.

Great Goddess on high, Simon was correct. The spotlight was so bright I couldn't see a single face in the audience. Unfortunately I couldn't see anything at all and narrowly missed walking right off the front of the stage and into the unsuspecting arms of a patron. Thankfully Chunk was quick on his feet and pulled me back from the edge.

I'd be at loathe to admit it later, but I was having fun. The more I got into it the better it was and the crowd was hooting, hollering and applauding like crazy. I knew some of the noise was the alcohol talking, but it was fun to pretend it was for me too.

Sassy ran out on the stage and joined me as my dad droned on about how Mommie was too vain to get fat and have children and decided to adopt as a publicity stunt.

Was that actually true?

"Joan and her children, Christina and Christopher, posed for many pictures in every popular magazine of the time!" Fabio's voice boomed through the speakers.

"Bob, get your beaver butt out here. We're on," Sassy hissed under her breath as Bob stood frozen in the wings refusing to move.

"To the world Christina and Christopher had the perfect life with their loving Mommie, but was that really what was going on?" Fabio's recording crooned.

"Bob you little butt-brain, get yourself and your unibrow out on this stage immediately," Sassy demanded in what kind-of sort-of passed as a loud stage whisper.

Bob was still frozen like a statue and going nowhere fast. Whatever. We could do it with out him. I gave Sassy my best Joan Crawford eyeball and pulled her attention back to me. We posed and smiled as Simon blinked the spotlight on and off as if it were a giant camera. I was literally seeing spots by the time we'd done all twenty-five poses.

Bob was still in the wings looking like he was going to hurl. I knew I could whip up a little magical wind and blow his sorry ass onto the stage, but since the costumes were *on loan* I didn't want Bob's bile to destroy them. I did this for Fabio to save him from going to jail. However, I also did it for myself because getting thrown up on wasn't on my agenda for the evening.

And then every actor's nightmare happened... or at least mine.

The audio went out. There was no more voice-over. No more Fabio telling the crowd about Joan's farked up life and what a shitty mother she was. Nope, there was nothing but silence.

Horrible, heinous silence.

My heart thundered in my chest and I was certain it could be heard in the next county. My mouth went dry and I felt ill. Should I poof away and never come back? No. That was a weenie move, but what in the heck was I supposed to do?

Sassy looked up at me with huge eyes. She was on her knees pretending to be ten year old Christina and was as thrown as I was. I vaguely heard my dad freaking out in the back of the house as he tried to fix the sound system. The audience was still with us, laughing and thinking this was part of the show. Drunk patrons were a huge blessing. Goddess bless Wanda and her Long Island ice tea.

But this wasn't part of the show—not even a little bit.

"Press the red button," I heard Simon shout to my dad over the loud ringing in my ears.

"Where in the hell is the red button? I can't see it," My dad shouted back.

"I got ya," Simon told him as he moved the beam from the spotlight off the stage to illuminate the back of the house so my dad could see.

This was bad—very bad. Not only was I on stage feeling more naked than if I was naked, I could now see everyone in the house—and they were staring at me... waiting.

Closing my eyes, I inhaled through my nose and blew it out slowly through my mouth. What doesn't kill you makes you stronger, according to Kelly Clarkson. I was a witch that could take out the continental USA with a blink of my eyes. I had popped hundreds of evil honey badgers and I could heal head wounds and ruptured spleens with my bare hands and magic. Why was standing on stage in front of intoxicated Shifters making me want to melt into the floor like the Wicked Witch of the West?

"What do we do?" Sassy whispered in a panic.

"Um… " I stuttered as I took in the sea of faces who were beginning to wonder what was going on.

I spotted Mac looking concerned, but as supportive as ever. His wave of encouragement was nice, but it wasn't his ass up on stage. It was mine and my daughter Christina's. Maybe I should just grab a stack of wire hangers and pass them out and it could become an interactive show. No. Bad idea. Wire hangers and sloshed Shifters equaled the loss of many eyeballs.

Fabio said to just make it up if something went wrong. I was good at creating fairy tales. Maybe I could do this too. I'd just leave the sex part out.

As my own internal panic attack continued, something oddly familiar and uncomfortable washed over me. I glanced out at the audience and my eyes landed on Baba Yaga who was smiling at me and urging me to continue. She was dressed like a Madonna extra from a 1980's music video. That didn't surprise me. Her taste was appalling, but she was always on my side. As much as I bitched about her, I knew she wanted the best for me. She was odd in her methodology, but she was consistent.

No, it wasn't Baba Yocray-cray that unsettled me, it was the woman seated next to her. Why was she here? Who on the Goddess's green earth thought that bringing her here was a good plan? Did my father know she was in the audience? I never thought I would lay eyes on the woman again in my life. The lead ball of fear in my stomach disintegrated and was replaced by butterflies of insecurity.

Slowly I walked to the edge of the stage keeping direct eye contact with the woman who bore me. She stared back with no expression on her face whatsoever. She wasn't angry or resentful. Was she happy to see me?

No. She wasn't happy. However, she wasn't trying to kill me either. She was somber and detached…

Sassy was breathing hard and mumbling to herself but I barely heard her ramblings as I was totally focused on my mother. I knew my pseudo daughter was talking, but I couldn't make out what she was saying. Everything in the room disappeared for me except my mother's emotionless face. And then I heard Sassy speak.

"Mommie," she cried out dramatically. "Why don't you love me? What did I do wrong?"

An unpleasant laugh left my lips as I realized the irony of what was unfolding. I'd asked the same horrible question repeatedly my entire life and had come up empty every time... but maybe tonight I could close the chapter.

Turning my back on my mother and the crowd, I looked at Sassy kneeling on the floor beseeching me to answer her. But I didn't see Sassy. I knew she was there, but she had turned into someone else—someone who wanted the same answer she did. I saw me as a little girl. I realized I had the chance to change history right in front of the woman who had burned my worthlessness into my brain. I could tell myself as a child that I was loved and cherished and that I was a lovable little witch.

My mother could take me in her arms and hug me and kiss me. She could tell me she was proud of me and that I would be a wonderful mother just like her some day. She could tell me that I was her good little girl and she would do absolutely anything for me.

It would be so perfect... but it would also be a lie.

Roger had made it clear that at a certain point, I had to make a choice. I could live in the past and let it shape my future or I could make my own future.

I was going to make my own future.

Right now.

"Christina, I don't love you," I said coldly in a voice I didn't know I possessed. Was Joan's spirit living in her freakin' clothes and was I channeling her?

"You don't?" Sassy whispered brokenly with very real tears in her eyes.

"No. I don't," I continued, looking away from her tear stained face that reminded me far too much of my own as a child. "You see, I'm not capable of loving you. I'm not capable of loving anyone. Maybe something happened in my life that hardened me or maybe I was so consumed with having power I forgot to care. It doesn't really matter, but you're correct. I don't love you."

A hush fell over the audience and the laughing and whispering ceased. They were riveted and had sobered up quickly.

"And as much as it may hurt you to know I don't love you, it's important that you accept it. Nothing you do will ever make me love you. I can't feel it and I don't want it. It means less than nothing to me. However, there is one thing that you should remember. It's probably the only real truth I will ever tell you." I paused and an eerie calm came over me. It was a feeling of closure and an omen of a new beginning.

Sassy stared at me in shock and I gave her a real Zelda smile. Her return smile went straight to my heart.

"It's not your fault that I don't love you. You did nothing wrong. Sometimes life doesn't follow natural order. Sometimes mothers don't love their daughters... but it's not your fault. I promise. It's not your fault."

The clapping started slowly and then became so frenzied I could feel it in my stomach like a bass drum. I didn't care. There was only one person I wanted to see and she was seated next to Baba Yaga.

I turned and raised my eyes to those of my mother. I didn't expect her to magically love me anymore. Her eyes held no more emotion than they had before my speech, but she gave me a gift. The most important gift she'd ever given me.

Without altering her expression, she nodded at me—once. It was small but it was very clear. I expected my heart to shatter into a million pieces, but it didn't. The emotion that consumed me was relief. It wasn't my fault. It had never been my fault. I was lovable, but just not to her. There was nothing I could have done to make her want me, but it didn't mean that others in my life would feel the same way.

Baba Yaga's posse of icky warlocks took my mother by the arm and escorted her to the exit as the Yaga watched the exchange between mother and daughter. The audience still roared, but I barely heard them. The most powerful witch of them all had a hand in this. I was certain of it. Baba Yobusybody meddled in everyone's lives. And right here, right now, I was grateful she had meddled in mine.

I didn't need therapy anymore... well, I didn't need it to deal with my Mommie issues anymore. Roger would be relieved to go back to once a week sessions. I was quite sure I needed head shrinking for about a million other things, but that was fine by me. I was by no means perfect, but the piece of me that I'd been searching for was now mine.

My father sobbed in the back of the house and the crowd jumped to their feet. The NASTY people were clapping louder that anyone in the theatre and I was thrilled for my dad. However, I was never doing another show again. Ever.

The play was over. Simon had been wrong. It only took fourteen minutes and twenty-two seconds, but we were a hit. Bob was still standing rooted to the floor in the wings, but he was clapping as wildly as the rest of the audience.

Sassy tackled me and peppered my face with kisses. "I think you might have healed something in my soul," she shouted over the cheering. "You really are my best friend in the world. I love you."

I laughed and pushed her off of me before she decided to hump me in gratitude. That would be a total downer and I wanted to end on a high note. And there was one more thing I needed to do.

I hopped up and searched the crowd for Mac. I didn't have to look far. He was standing right in front of me. There were so many things I wanted to say, but only one thing came out.

"I love you, Mac."

His grin made me weak. He scooped me up in his arms and hugged me so tight I thought I might break. "I know you do, pretty girl. I'm just glad you figured it out. My Bon Jovi has been in tremendous amounts of pain lately."

"I suppose we could do a little something about that," I purred with a sly grin and a giggle.

"Zelda," Fabio screamed as he rushed the stage and yanked me out of Mac's arms. "You were brilliant. I am so proud of you. Look at me! I'm still crying. I love you so much!"

"I love you too, Dad." I kissed his cheek and laid my head on his chest.

"You *must* meet the NASTY people. They are positively raving about you. I'm certain you're going to be up for a national award for this. Come, come, come," he said as he pulled me away from Mac.

Mac just smiled and nodded. "I'll wait for you forever," he said. "Go greet your adoring fans."

"You don't have to wait forever. You have me now," I promised as I followed my dad into the crazy crowd.

I was happy. I was a lovable witch. No longer was I waiting for the other shoe to drop.

However, that's when it usually did.

CHAPTER 18

The crowds had left and most of the cast had gone to the Assjacket Diner for the after party. There were only a few of us left cleaning up at the Community Center. The NASTY gang had been impressed and promised a great review along with attendance at all of my father's future productions. Fabio literally preened and held Baba Yaga's hand the entire time.

They were certainly a pair, but I was good with it. I wanted my dad to be happy and if happy meant dating an eighties reject with more power in her little pinkie than all the witches I knew put together, then so be it. Maybe my dad would lighten the Yagahiney up. Stranger things had happened.

Sassy, Jeeves and the chipmunks were hugging and giggling. Mac stood with my fat cats and gazed at me with pride and desire. I was definitely hitting the tree house tonight. It was time to let my hair down and get laid.

"Baba darling, do you know of a warlock or genie named Ber?" Fabio asked as he played with her Bo Derrick braids.

It was a good question. Baba Yaga knew everyone. We needed to pay Ber off and get Chutney back—the sooner the better.

"A genie?" she pondered aloud as she tapped her long, highly manicured nails on her swath of black rubber arm bracelets. "No, I can't think of a genie named Ber."

"Might be a lesbian," Fat Bastard chimed in unhelpfully.

"I'm sorry. What?" Baba Yaga asked, confused.

"Ignore him," I told her. "What about a warlock?"

"Well, if Ber is a nick name, I can only think of one and he practices very dark magic," she told us with a shudder of disgust.

The Chipmunks scurried over with wide eyes and jaws working. Sassy and Jeeves also joined the conversation. Mac stepped up next to me and the cats flanked my feet.

"Hesabadbadbadbadbadman," Chunk cried out as he stood close to his brothers.

"If you're speaking of Bermangoggleshitz, then you're right my little one," Baba said as she absently patted him on the head.

"What in the frackin' hell kind of name is Bermangoggleshitz?" Fat Bastard demanded laughing so hard he fell on his fat kitty ass.

"Great Goddess in a tutu," Fabio hissed as his eyes narrowed to slits. "Don't laugh. That son of a bitch is dangerous."

"Fabio is correct," Baba Yaga concurred. "Why are we even discussing the horrible man?"

"Do you want to explain or should I?" I asked the chipmunks.

All three chipmunks had passed out cold. Clearly we'd nailed the name on the head. However, relaying the circumstances to Baba Yaga was going to be a challenge.

"Suffice it to say the chipmunks owe him money. He's holding their brother hostage. I'm going to pay him off for the gum-smacking idiots and Sassy and Jeeves are going to adopt them while they work off what they owe," I told her.

"We're keeping them even after they work off the two hundred grand," Sassy chimed in.

"Interesting," Baba Yaga said as she approached me.

I backed up just in case I'd said something she didn't like.

"You're using your own money to do this?" she asked in a deadly quiet voice.

"Um, yes," I whispered in reply as I racked my brain to figure out if there was some random ass magical rule against paying off gambling debts of chipmunks.

She was silent for about fourteen seconds too long. I started to sweat... and then I got pissed. Wait. This was bullshit. It was *my* money—albeit inherited. I could do whatever I wanted with it. Baba YomyrealnameisCarol could bite my ass. I liked the stupid unconscious chipmunks and I wanted to help.

"I don't care what the rules are, Carol," I snapped as I got in her face. "And I don't care if you don't like it. I'm the damn Shifter Wanker here and I'm keeping my people safe. It's my money and... "

"Goddess, you're going to be a wonderful Baba Yaga when your time comes!" she shouted gleefully as she wrapped her arms around me and hugged me lovingly.

"Thank you," I muttered as I spit one of her braids out of my mouth. "Wait. What the *fuck*?" I screeched as I wiggled out of her grasp.

"I haven't told her yet, darling," Fabio said as he pulled Baba Yaga back just in case I started swinging.

"Whoops," she trilled. "Surprise!"

Yep, it was a surprise and not a welcome one. Now I knew what the cats and my dad had been discussing when I was spying on them. I was barely used to being the damn Shifter Wanker. Becoming the next Baba Yaga was not on my list of things to do in this lifetime.

"You're not retiring any time soon?" I questioned the nut job in charge.

"No, my young witch," Baba promised. "You've got a long way to go before I can retire in good conscience."

"Thank the Goddess for that," Sassy commented loudly.

I shot her a glare that made her step behind Jeeves. As much as I agreed with the sentiment, I was the only one allowed to speak it.

"So are you saying this Bermangoggleshitz is not a lesbian?" Fat Bastard inquired still cackling over the ridiculous name.

"Oh shit," Sassy screeched as the room filled with an acrid green smoke. "That was the third time, you dumb ass. You've conjured the lesbian."

"So he *is* a lesbian?" the Bastard choked out as the smoke filled his lungs.

The walls of the Community Center rocked ominously and threatened to cave in. Black snakes slithered across the floor and hissed at us. Mac picked up the chipmunks and tossed them to safety up in the rafters and then quickly put me and the cats on a table. Sassy grabbed Jeeves and levitated above the hungry serpents as Mac shifted and began tearing them to shreds.

"Damn it," Baba Yaga snarled as she and my father floated up above the fray. "Bermangoggleshitz has to be battled with dark magic."

"I don't have black magic," Fabio growled as he shot deadly red fire at the snakes.

"Neither do I," Baba said way too calmly, considering vipers were now climbing the walls. "But someone here does."

Son. Of. A. Bitch. I had dark magic compliments of my mother. I'd never used it, but I supposed there was no time like the present to try it out.

"Someone summoned me?" Bermangoggleshitz said in a flat bored tone.

I'd never seen anything like him in my life. He was huge and had horns. His hair matched his eyes, which were as black as night and he smelled like shit on a stick. Goddess, was this what dark magic did to a witch? Would I turn into an abomination if I used mine? Would any of us make it out of here alive if I didn't give the evil sorcery a try? Shitshitshit.

You'd think having to play Joan Crawford would have been enough for a gal, now this?

"It was an accident," I said trying to reason with the nightmare before I had to attempt blowing his ass up.

"I don't believe in accidents," he bellowed. "I sense the ones that owe me money. Give me my money," he roared.

"Not so fast, Bermangogglestinkyshitz," I shouted back as I levitated off the table and floated toward him.

"What did you just call me?" he demanded.

"Bermangoggleshitz," I replied with an innocent smile.

"No you didn't," he said as his eyes squinted to beady slits.

"Yep, I did," I shot back, thinking that my maturity level wasn't serving me well at the moment. "And you'll get your money when I get Chutney back."

"I ate him," he purred and then belched.

"What?" I shouted as black flames shot from my hands.

He'd had eaten poor Chutney? He was not getting his money and he wasn't leaving alive.

"I'm kidding," he hissed with a chuckle that made me want to heave.

"Your sense of humor sucks," I snapped as I held up my hands so he could see he had some competition—at least I prayed he did. I had no clue what I was doing, but bluffing was second nature.

"Tell me something I don't know," he muttered as he waved his hand and Chutney appeared coughing and chewing gum frantically.

"Money?" Bermangoggleshitz inquired as he gripped Chutney by the neck.

My father snapped his fingers and a large wad of cash appeared in my hands.

"Get rid of the snakes, hand over Chutney and you'll get your money," I instructed tersely as Mac growled beneath me on the floor.

"Did you bring interest?" the abomination asked as he bared sharp teeth at me.

"Did you come here to get what's owed to you or did come here to get your ass kicked?" I snarled as I pointed at his head and let a small zap fly—at least I thought it was going to be small.

A glittering bolt of black magic darted from my fingertips and blasted Bermangoggleshitz into the back wall of the Center with a sickening thud. He dropped the screaming Chutney in his shock and fury. Mac, in his wolf form caught the chipmunk and dragged him to relative safety.

"Who are you?" Bermangoggleshitz bellowed as he recovered and came right for me.

"Blow the lesbian up," Fat Bastard grunted as my cats formed a semi-circle in front of me.

"Everyone take cover," I yelled as I wound up and flew right at the evil freight train that was gunning for me.

We both stopped mere inches from each other. My insides churned, but outwardly I displayed calm. I was really glad I'd told Mac how I felt. I'd hate to bite it without him knowing that I loved him.

"You want your money or do you want a piece of me, you stinky assbucket?" I snapped as my upper body began to smolder in swirls of black glitter.

"Again," he ground out. "Who are you?"

"I'm the Shifter Wanker and you're in my territory. I've had a really bad day and you're not helping my mood. I'm tired, hungry and I need to get laid. If I have to turn you to dust to accomplish that, so be it. You can take your money and leave or I can keep your money and Chutney and send you back to hell. Your choice."

I prayed to the Goddess and every deity I could think of that Bermangoggleshitz would take the money and run during our twenty-seven second stare down. I had no idea if I could take him out, but I knew I would die trying if I had to.

"You amuse me, little Shifter Wanker and your dark magic is strong—if untrained. Today I think I will simply take my money and leave. However, we shall meet again. Eventually you will need me," he said as he held out his calloused hand for the cash.

"Don't bet on it, Bermangagmeshitz," I shot back evenly and handed him the money.

"But I'm a gambling man," he informed me with a laugh so hideous I blanched. "Till we meet again."

With that, Bermangoggleshitz poofed away taking his snakes and his stench with him. I dropped to the floor and curled into a ball. Mac shifted back and took me into his strong arms.

"Is everyone okay?" I asked, shaking like a leaf.

"Yes, we are," Baba Yaga said as she stroked my hair. "You might be ready sooner than I thought."

"No," Mac growled, starring daggers at Baba Yaga. "She's got enough on her plate right now. Leave her alone."

"It's not my choice to make," Baba snapped in a voice would give all of us nightmares for a couple weeks. "And you're being insolent."

"My apologies," Mac said with respect. "But she's only thirty. Let her live a normal life for a while."

"It's okay," I told Mac as I stood and faced the leader of the witches. "I'm not ready yet. I have no clue if I could have taken that freak show out. I was bluffing."

"He knew that," she commented mildly.

"And he let me live?"

"He knows as well as I do how powerful you will become and now you owe him a favor. Bermangoggleshitz may be evil, but he is not stupid. However, the chipmunks are another story," Baba Yoscary said as she turned her attention to the rodents. "How did you get involved with the warlock?"

"He seemed really nice at first," Chad offered up with an embarrassed shrug.

Baba's eye roll beat all the eye rolls I'd witnessed in my short life. "Sassy, can you handle these simpletons and teach them good from evil?"

"Yes, I can. I will also smite their asses if they get out of line," Sassy replied as she stood proud and tall. "I will be a good mother."

"I believe you will." Baba Yaga sighed as she took my father's hand in hers and leaned on him. "Fabio, I'd like to go to Paris. I need some crème brulee and a good bottle of red. Can you arrange that?"

"Your wish is my command, darling," he said, kissing the top of her braided head.

"Zelda, I'm proud of you. You deserve some peace. However, I shall be watching. Always," Baba Yaga warned in her *I am the ruler of the world* voice.

Fabio crossed to me and took my face gently in his hands. "Are you really okay, my sweet? What you did tonight was nothing short of amazing and I'm not talking about the play."

"I am," I told him truthfully. "As awful as it was, it needed to be done. And just so you know... I love you."

"And I you," my dad said as he pressed his lips to my forehead. "I'm assuming this means I'll be getting a new son-in-law?"

"Possibly," I mumbled as I felt heat crawl up my neck.

"Yes," Mac corrected me. "You will."

"That's all kinds of hot," Sassy cheered as she pulled her still shell-shocked new family toward the exit. "I want all the details, bestie!"

"Well, we're off," Fabio announced as he and Baba Yobearerofscarynews poofed off to Paris.

"So I take it Bermangoggleshitz is not a lesbian?" Fat Bastard asked as he, Boba Fett and Jango Fett waddled after Sassy and her crew.

"Correct," I muttered with a stifled chuckle, hoping we were done with the ambiguous sexual references for a while.

"It's still a shitty name," Jango grunted as he grabbed the plungers from the prop table and followed the group.

I had to agree. It was a shitty name, but in the end it had not been a shitty night—not at all.

"You ready to christen the tree house?" Mac asked with a sexy lopsided grin.

"Yes. Yes, I believe I am."

CHAPTER 19

"Why do I feel like a virgin on her wedding night?" I blurted out as I glanced around the charming tree house with delight.

The interior was as lovely as the exterior. It was one large, open room dominated by a king sized bed—definitely a sex pad. The colors were light and airy and all of the windows were open letting in the cool evening breeze. My stomach clenched in nervousness and excitement. I was going to do this.

"You *are* a virgin on your wedding night," Mac replied as he set an enormous cooler full of food down next to the bed.

"I'm *not* a virgin." I giggled as I hopped on the bed and bounced. Little sparkles of golden magic danced around the room as my joy overwhelmed me. "And we're not getting married."

"You're a virgin to the Mating Frenzy," he commented as he grinned with pure masculine satisfaction and caught some of the glittering enchantment on his fingers.

"So are you," I reminded him feeling a little possessive. He was mine now.

"Yep." His grin grew wider and he stripped off his clothes so fast my head spun. "And mating is far more bonding than marriage."

"For Shifters," I reminded him as I admired his hot bod and tried not to drool.

"For us," he corrected as he sat on the edge of the bed and took my hands in his. "Zelda, we don't have to mate tonight if it's too soon for you. We can make love till the sun comes up and go slowly with the till death do us part section."

"I love you," I whispered meaning it even though the thought of mating still unnerved me.

"And I love you. We're mates, but this has been a long and emotional day. If you're not ready, I'll wait."

As I searched his eyes I knew he was serious. Goddess, he was all kinds of perfect. I was terrified, but did I want to wait? The simple fact that he insisted on it as an option even though he was a bossy, alpha-male, he-man made me love him even more. The bite was probably going to suck, but I'd dealt with plenty of pain in my life. What exactly was I scared of?

I loved him.

He loved me.

I was certain I wanted to spend the rest of my long *not boring* life with him.

He was good inside and out.

He would be a great father for puppies, which I was still concerned I would blow out.

He thought my crazy was sexy.

He had an ass to die for and a very *fine* Bon Jovi.

I was in—all in.

"I don't want to wait. Bite me, wolfman," I said on a single breath as I tore my clothes off and jumped him.

"You're sure?" he asked as his fangs dropped and his body hardened underneath mine.

His eyes glowed with desire and love as he gently laid me back on the bed. Millions of thoughts of ways to tell him I loved him swirled through my brain, but all I could do was nod.

"It will only hurt for a second," he whispered as his fangs scraped the soft skin of my neck.

I shuddered and moaned then pressed even closer to his body. Every part of me felt like a live wire. Goddess, the anticipation was hotter than hell, I wondered if the bite would make me explode.

"How does it work?" I gasped out, wriggling like a cat in heat against him.

"I think it will come naturally." His warm breath tickled my neck sending me into a mini orgasm.

How on earth did he do that? He'd barely touched me and I was already having mini explosions. As his hands began to roam my naked body, I arched into them. There was no possible way to get close enough.

"Should we just do it fast and get it over with?" I asked breathlessly as I ran my hands greedily over his broad shoulders and chest.

"Never done this before so I'm not sure," he mumbled as his mouth began to trace the path that his hands had just taken.

Oh. My. Goddess. His lips found my aching breasts and tingles shot through my body right to Little Red Riding Hood. Mac's hand caught my wrists and trapped them above my head as he went back to work.

I dragged air into my lungs and tried to think, but my mind was a blur of pleasure and need. My breathing grew ragged as his open mouth slid lower. All rational thought ceased.

"So fucking hot," he whispered against my skin.

My hips rocked and his growl of lust sent chills through me. His wolf, as close to the surface as I'd ever seen it, sent my body into overdrive. Mac's mouth found the spot that made coherent anything impossible and I whimpered and writhed.

Just as I was about to detonate he stopped abruptly and eased his way back up my body. His eyes were unfocused and he was close to going over the edge. I felt bold and fearless. The power I held over this beautiful man was only matched by the power he had over me. In his arms was exactly where I wanted to be. I'd never been so sure about anything in my entire life.

I slowly ran my tongue over the seam of his mouth and tangled my fingers in his thick hair. Pulling him closer, I nipped and bit at his full lips.

"The next time you come will be with me buried inside you," he informed me with hooded eyes and a wicked sexy smirk.

My magic burst in little golden bubbles and rained down on us as my use of language still eluded me. Mac's laugh of delight made my heart tighten in happiness.

"Goddess," I heaved out on an uneven breath. "The Mating Frenzy rocks."

"Baby, the Mating Frenzy hasn't even started yet."

"Oh shit."

I felt his hardness on my thigh and heard his harsh intake of breath as I guided him into me. I moaned as he pushed and my body softened to accommodate him.

"Holy hell," I hissed as he continued to move. "Did Bon Jovi get bigger?"

"He's anticipating the frenzy." Mac groaned and every muscle in his body went taut. "I'll go slow," he promised gruffly. "Tell me if it hurts."

"It hurts good," I hissed as I rotated my hips taking as much as I could. He was very well endowed on a good day, but this was freakin' awesome.

"I'm so in love with you," he ground out as his hips jerked and he buried himself to the hilt. "You're mine."

Stars ripped across my vision and my body jerked uncontrollably beneath his. His sharp fangs grazed my shoulder as his body moved in rhythm with mine. Need consumed me like I'd never known and I grabbed his head and pressed his mouth to my neck.

He needed no more invitation.

The sound of fangs puncturing skin should have been gross, but it was hotter than Hell in July. Mac's scent and the sexy sounds coming from deep in his chest undid me. Stark need—naked desire. I screamed at the animalistic invasion and then sobbed as I came harder than I ever had in my life. The burning made me go rigid for a brief moment, but the sheer pleasure that roared through my body replaced the pain quickly.

Mac's body trembled as we performed a ritual more magical than any spell I'd ever cast. We belonged to each other for eternity and nothing would undo our vow. It was as exhilarating as it was terrifying, but it was so right.

I thought I loved him before. That was nothing compared to how I felt now.

"More," he demanded as he pulled out, flipped me to my stomach then entered me again.

The aftershocks of my orgasm continued as a stronger one consumed me… and he didn't stop.

Nope, he went all night long and I went happily with him.

Oxygen wasn't necessary as we went from position to position that should have put both of us in traction for a year. The bed broke in half after one acrobatic go 'round so we just yanked the mattress off and continued on the floor.

It was all kinds of crazy and every kind of hot.

I wasn't sure if I would live through the night, but it was a hell of a way to go.

***

"I think I came fifteen times," I purred happily as I lay like a wet noodle next to the greatest lover the Goddess ever created.

"You came twenty-one times," Mac corrected me as he grinned with well deserved cocky male satisfaction.

"I half expected to wake up in the Next Adventure this morning. I can't believe we lived through that." I giggled and snuggled up to him.

"You woke up exactly where you're supposed to. In my arms and in my bed—well, on my mattress on the floor," he informed me as we both took in the splintered king sized wooden frame with glee.

"I feel kind of funny," I mused aloud as I touched the bite mark on my neck. It was sore, but I liked it. "Will this leave a scar?"

"Nope," he said as he hopped up and started unloading the food from the cooler. "You hungry?"

"Dumb question," I said, sitting up and then falling right back down as dizziness overtook me.

Mac continued to pull out food, unaware that I wasn't quite right. I kicked him in his naked butt with my foot to get his attention.

"Something's wonky," I told him as I tried to sit up again only to lie right back down. "I feel weird."

"You're just hungry," he said avoiding eye contact.

"I'm always hungry," I snapped.

Why was he being evasive and a dick? We'd just had the best sex-a-thon of our lives and he was frantically yanking bagels and cream cheese out of a cooler. Oh. My.

Goddess. Was I going to turn into a wolf? Did he leave out some pertinent information? I liked being a witch. I did *not* want to go furry on full moons.

"You just need some protein and you'll be right as rain," he said nervously as he slapped ten hardboiled eggs on a plate and put it in front of me.

"Right as rain?" I repeated with narrowed eyes. "Did you turn into my dad?"

"Um … no," he replied as he began to straighten the room. "Eat. You need your energy."

"Because I'm going to turn into a wolf?" I hissed as I yet again tried to sit up.

I had more success this time, but I was still strangely shaky.

"No, of course not." His laugh was hearty, but he was still in avoidance mode. "You have to be *born* a wolf."

"Interesting," I commented as I inhaled the eggs and the bagels as if I hadn't eaten in a month. "I'm still hungry."

"On it," he said as he unloaded fruit, coffee cake and pickles from the cooler.

I grabbed the pickles and shoved them into my mouth followed by half the coffee cake and then went right back to the pickles. Damn, pickles and coffee cake were a delicious combo.

"Did you bring ice cream or raw steak or maybe some bones to chew on?" I asked with a mouthful and then froze.

Bones to chew on? What in the Goddesses name was wrong with me? I didn't eat raw steak and I'd never gnawed on a bone in my life. Mac was now cleaning windows like his life depended on it and had worked up a sweat. It was kind of hot to see a sexy dude doing housework, but the windows were already spotless. The wolf had some explaining to do.

"You wanna help me out here?" I asked him as the truth I was firmly in denial of began to dawn on me.

"Sure," he said as he grabbed an enormous raw steak and six bones out of the cooler and shoved them onto my hands.

"You knew I'd want this?" I shrieked in disbelief as my mouth watered at the disgusting pile of formerly inedible food in my lap.

"I thought there was a possibility," he admitted sheepishly as he backed away cautiously.

"Of ...?" I questioned with narrowed eyes, knowing the answer but unsure I could hear it without passing out.

"Of us making a baby," he mumbled and quickly raised the raw steak to my lips.

I ate it as my brain and my emotions ping-ponged around like a spray of bullets from a machine gun. This was not possible. I just figured out I could love people and accept their love. I'd broken a bed during a sex marathon with a man who turns into a wolf. I call my woowoo Little Red Riding Hood. I couldn't be anyone's mother. I was a materialistic Shifter Wanker who used profanity in my spells.

I had no clue how to change diapers or weave fairy tales without sex in them. Taking care of *cats* was a challenge for me. How in the hell was I supposed to raise a baby? I was a magical, irresponsible, walking clusterfuck in Prada wedges. Tears blurred my eyes as I thought of all the ways I would unintentionally screw up my kid.

I didn't deserve a baby.

"It doesn't usually happen this quickly," Mac said in a rush as he took me in his arms and held me close. "I felt the magic in the air, but I was so blinded with lust and love that I pushed it aside."

"You knew?" I accused and tried unsuccessfully to pull away. His arms felt so good, but I was torn with fear and confusion.

"Kind of," he admitted. "I'm sorry I didn't stop or say something, but I'm not sorry you're carrying our child. This baby was created in love and I already love her—completely."

My tears increased and I could hear the rain pattering on the roof of the tree house. The scent of blooms filled the air. I stood and walked numbly to the window.

Riotous color greeted my eyes and the sun shone bright making the meadow appear to be a painting so beautiful it was unreal. A glorious rainbow shot across the sky and bursts of pink and blue glittering magic shimmered through the raindrops.

The Goddess was sending me a message. There were no mistakes in life. Not even my loveless childhood was a mistake. I wouldn't be who I was standing here right now if I hadn't gone through what I had. I would have never met Mac or become the Shifter Wanker. I wouldn't have run over my dad and spent nine months in the pokey with my annoying best friend, Sassy. I wouldn't have starred in a heinous play... and I wouldn't be pregnant.

I should have figured I'd be one of those girls that got knocked up on her wedding night—for lack of a more accurate term.

My tears still flowed but for an entirely different reason. I was going to be a real mommy. I was going to be a *good* mommy who loved her children and kissed them so often it would be embarrassing. I would rewrite the sad chapters of my book and make them wonderful for my children.

And the shopping... I was going to be great at that part. Baby clothes are freakin' adorable. My kids will be the best-dressed kids alive.

"It's not a girl," I said quietly and turned to look at the man who was going to be an amazing father.

"It's not?" he asked as he watched me with so much love in his eyes I was humbled.

"Well, it is," I whispered as a small smile pulled at my lips. "But there's a little boy in there too."

"How do you know?" he asked as he crossed the room and gathered me in his arms.

Glancing over my shoulder I peeked at the pink and blue magic that floated toward me on the breeze and I grinned. "The Goddess told me."

"We're having two babies?" he whispered as he laid his hands protectively over my stomach.

"Yep," I said as I placed my hands reverently over his. "We're gonna a have litter."

Roger was right. Life was not boring—terrifying maybe—but not boring. I held on tight to the father of my children—or my puppies. That still remained to be seen.

"I'll eat more than usual," I warned him.

"Goddess help us all," he said with a chuckle as he buried his face in my hair and gently rubbed my stomach. "We're going to be good parents, Zelda."

"Yes, we are," I said, closing my eyes and silently thanking the Goddess for leading me to this place in time. "We are going to be the best parents ever."

And I knew with all my heart I was telling the truth.

However, we had to get through the pregnancy first.

The End... for now #

NOTE FROM THE AUTHOR

If you enjoyed this book, please consider leaving a positive review or rating on the site where you purchased it. Reader reviews help my books continue to be valued by retailers and help new readers make decisions about reading them. You are the reason I write these stories and I sincerely appreciate each of you!

Many thanks for your support,

~ Robyn Peterman

Want to hear about my new releases? Visit my website at **www.robynpeterman.com** and join my mailing list!

EXCERPT FROM *READY TO WERE*

SHIFT HAPPENS SERIES Book One

BOOK DESCRIPTION

I never planned on going back to Hung Island, Georgia. Ever.

I was a top notch Were agent for the secret paranormal Council and happily living in Chicago where I had everything I needed – a gym membership, season tickets to the Cubs and Dwayne – my gay, Vampyre best friend. Going back now would mean facing the reason I'd left and I'd rather chew my own paw off than deal with Hank.

Hank the Tank Wilson was the six foot three, obnoxious, egotistical, perfect-assed, best-sex-of-my-life, Werewolf who cheated on me and broke my heart. At the time, I did what any rational woman would do. I left in the middle of the night with a suitcase, big plans and enough money for a one-way bus ticket to freedom. I vowed to never return.

But here I am, trying to wrap my head around what has happened to some missing Weres without wrapping my body around Hank. I hope I don't have to eat my words and my paw.

***This novella originally appeared in the *Three Southern Beaches* collection released July of 2014. This is an extended version of that story.

CHAPTER 1

"You're joking."

"No, actually I'm not," my boss said and slapped the folder into my hands. "You leave tomorrow morning and I don't want to see your hairy ass till this is solved."

I looked wildly around her office for something to lob at her head. It occurred to me that might not be the best of ideas, but desperate times led to stupid measures. She could not do this to me. I'd worked too hard and I wasn't going back. Ever.

"First of all, my ass is not hairy except on a full moon and you're smoking crack if you think I'm going back to Georgia."

Angela crossed her arms over her ample chest and narrowed her eyes at me. "Am I your boss?" she asked.

"Is this a trick question?"

She huffed out an exasperated sigh and ran her hands through her spiked 'do making her look like she'd been electrocuted. "Essie, I am cognizant of how you feel about Hung Island, Georgia, but there's a disaster of major proportions on the horizon and I have no choice."

"Where are you sending Clark and Jones?" I demanded.

"New York and Miami."

"Oh my god," I shrieked. "Who did I screw over in a former life that those douches get to go to cool cities and I have to go home to an island called Hung?"

"Those douches *do* have hairy asses and not just on a full moon. You're the only female agent I have that looks like a model so you're going to Georgia. Period."

"Fine. I'll quit. I'll open a bakery."

Angela smiled and an icky feeling skittered down my spine. "Excellent, I'll let you tell the Council that all the money they invested in your training is going to be flushed down the toilet because you want to bake cookies."

The Council consisted of supernaturals from all sorts of species. The branch that currently had me by the metaphorical balls was WTF—Werewolf Treaty Federation. They were the worst as far as stringent rules and consequences went. The Vampyres were loosey goosey, the Witches were nuts and the freakin' Fairies were downright pushovers, but not the Weres. Nope, if you enlisted you were in for life. It had sounded so good when the insanely sexy recruiting officer had come to our local Care For Your Inner Were meeting.

Training with the best of the best. Great salary with benefits. Apartment and company car. But the kicker for me was that it was fifteen hours away from the hell I grew up in. No longer was I Essie from Hung Island, Georgia— *and who in their right mind would name an island Hung*—I was Agent Essie McGee of the Chicago WTF. The irony of the initials was a source of pain to most Werewolves, but went right over the Council's heads due to the simple fact that they were older than dirt and oblivious to pop culture.

Yes, I'd been disciplined occasionally for mouthing off to superiors and using the company credit card for shoes, but other than that I was a damn good agent. I'd graduated at the top of my class and was the go-to girl for messy and dangerous assignments that no one in their right mind would take... I'd singlehandedly brought down three rogue Weres who were selling secrets to the Dragons—another supernatural species. The Dragons shunned the Council, had their own little club and a psychotic desire to rule the world. Several times they'd come close due to the fact that they were loaded and Weres from the New Jersey Pack were easily bribed. Not to mention the fire-breathing thing...

I was an independent woman living in the Windy City. I had a gym membership, season tickets to the Cubs and a gay Vampyre best friend named Dwayne. What more did a girl need?

Well, possibly sex, but the *bastard* had ruined me for other men...

Hank "The Tank" Wilson was the main reason I'd rather chew my own paw off than go back to Hung Island, Georgia. Six foot three of obnoxious, egotistical, perfect-assed, alpha male Werewolf. As the alpha of my local Pack he had decided it was high time I got mated...to him. I, on the other hand, had plans—big ones and they didn't include being barefoot and pregnant at the beck and call of a player.

So I did what any sane, rational woman would do. I left in the middle of the night with a suitcase, a flyer from the hot recruiter and enough money for a one-way bus ticket to freedom. Of course, nothing ever turns out as planned... The apartment was the size of a shoe box, the car was used and smelled like French fries and the benefits didn't kick in till I turned one hundred and twenty five. We Werewolves had long lives.

"Angela, you really can't do this to me." Should I get down on my knees? I was so desperate I wasn't above begging.

"Why? What happened there, Essie? Were you in some kind of trouble I should know about?" Her eyes narrowed, but she wasn't yelling.

I think she liked me...kind of. The way a mother would like an annoying spastic two year old who belonged to someone else.

"No, not exactly," I hedged. "It's just that..."

"Weres are disappearing and presumed dead. Considering no one knows of our existence besides other supernaturals, we have a problem. Furthermore, it seems like humans might be involved."

My stomach lurched and I grabbed Angela's office chair for balance. "Locals are missing?" I choked out. My grandma Bobby Sue was still there, but I'd heard from her last night. She'd harangued me about getting my belly button pierced. Why I'd put that on Instagram was beyond me. I was gonna hear about that one for the next eighty years or so.

"Not just missing—more than likely dead. Check the folder," Angela said and poured me a shot of whiskey.

With trembling hands I opened the folder. This had to be a joke. I felt ill. I'd gone to high school with Frankie Mac and Jenny Packer. Jenny was as cute as a button and was the cashier at the Piggly Wiggly. Frankie Mac had been the head cheerleader and cheated on every test since the fourth grade. Oh my god, Debbie Swink? Debbie Swink had been voted most likely to succeed and could do a double backwards flip off the high dive. She'd busted her head open countless times before she'd perfected it. Her mom was sure she'd go to the Olympics.

"I know these girls," I whispered.

"Knew. You knew them. They all were taking classes at the modeling agency."

"What modeling agency? There's no modeling agency on Hung Island." I sifted through the rest of the folder with a knot the size of a cantaloupe in my stomach. More names and faces I recognized. Sandy Moongie? *Wait a minute.*

"Um, not to speak ill of the dead, but Sandy Moongie was the size of a barn...she was modeling?"

"Worked the reception desk." Angela shook her head and dropped down on the couch.

"This doesn't seem that complicated. It's fairly black and white. Whoever is running the modeling agency is the perp."

"The modeling agency is Council sponsored."

I digested that nugget in silence for a moment.

"And the Council is running a modeling agency, why?"

"Word is that we're heading toward revealing ourselves to the humans and they're trying to find the most attractive representatives to do so."

"That's a joke, right?" *What kind of dumb ass plan was that?*

"I wish it was." Angela picked up my drink and downed it. "I'm getting too old for this shit," she muttered as she refilled the shot glass, thought better of it and just swigged from the bottle.

"Is the Council aware that I'm going in?"

"What do you think?"

"I think they're old and stupid and that they send in dispensable agents like me to clean up their shitshows," I grumbled.

"Smart girl."

"Who else knows about this? Clark? Jones?"

"They know," she said wearily. "They're checking out agencies in New York and Miami."

"Isn't it conflict of interest to send me where I know everyone?"

"It is, but you'll be able to infiltrate and get in faster that way. Besides, no one has disappeared from the other agencies yet."

There was one piece I still didn't understand. "How are humans involved?"

She sighed and her head dropped back onto her broad shoulders. "Humans are running the agency."

It took a lot to render me silent, like learning my grandma had been a stripper in her youth, and that all male Werewolves were hung like horses... but this was horrific.

"Who in the hell thought that was a good idea? My god, half the female Weres I know sprout tails when flash bulbs go off. We won't have to come out, they can just run billboards of hot girls with hairy appendages coming out of their asses."

"It's all part of the *Grand Plan*. If the humans see how wonderful and attractive we are, the issue of knowingly living alongside of us will be moot."

Again. Speechless.

"When are Council elections?" It was time to vote some of those turd knockers out.

"Essie." Angela rolled her eyes and took another swig. "There are no elections. They're appointed and serve for life."

"I knew that," I mumbled. Skipping Were History class was coming back to bite me in the butt.

"I'll go." There was no way I couldn't. Even though my knowledge of the hierarchy of my race was fuzzy, my skills were top notch and trouble seemed to find me. In any other job that would suck, but in mine, it was an asset.

"Good. You'll be working with the local Pack alpha. He's also the sheriff there. Name's Hank Wilson. You know him?"

"Yep." *Biblically. I knew the son of a bitch biblically.*

***

"You're gonna bang him."

"I am not gonna bang him."

"You are so gonna bang him."

"Dwayne, if I hear you say that I'm gonna bang him one more time, I will not let you borrow my black Mary Jane pumps. Ever again."

Dwayne made the international "zip the lip and throw away the key" sign while silently mouthing that I was going to bang Hank.

"I think you should bang him if he's a hot as you said." Dwayne made himself comfortable on my couch and turned on the TV.

"When did I ever say he was hot?" I demanded as I took the remote out of his hands. I was not watching any more *Dance Moms*. "I never said he was hot."

"Paaaaleese," Dwayne flicked his pale hand over his shoulder and rolled his eyes.

"What was that?"

"What was what?" he asked, confused.

"That shoulder thing you just did."

"Oh, I was flicking my hair over my shoulder in a *girlfriend* move."

"Okay, don't do that. It doesn't work. You're as bald as a cue ball."

"But it's the new move," he whined.

Oh my god, Vampyres were such high maintenance. "According to who?" I yanked my suitcase out from under my bed and started throwing stuff in.

"Kim Kardashian."

179

I refused to dignify that with so much as a look.

"Fine," he huffed. "But if you say one word about my skinny jeans I am so out of here."

I considered it, but I knew he was serious. As crazy as he drove me, I adored him. He was my only real friend in Chicago and I had no intention of losing him.

"I know he's hot," Dwayne said. "Look at you—you're so gorge it's redonkulous. You're all legs and boobs and hair and lips—you're far too beautiful to be hung up on a goober."

"Are you calling me shallow?" I snapped as I ransacked my tiny apartment for clean clothes. Damn it, tomorrow was laundry day. I was going to have to pack dirty clothes.

"So he's ugly and puny and wears bikini panties?"

"No! He's hotter than Satan's underpants and he wears boxer briefs," I shouted. "You happy?"

"He's actually a nice guy."

"You've met Hank?" I was so confused I was this close to making fun of his skinny jeans just so he would leave.

"Satan. He's not as bad as everyone thinks."

How was it that everyone I came in contact with today stole my ability to speak? Thankfully, I was interrupted by a knock at my door.

"You expecting someone?" Dwayne asked as he pilfered the remote back and found *Dance Moms*.

"No."

I peeked through the peephole. Nobody came to my place except Dwayne and the occasional pizza delivery guy or Chinese food take out guy or Indian food take out guy. *Wait. What the hell was my boss doing here?*

"Angela?"

"You going to let me in?"

"Depends."

"Open the damn door."

I did.

Angela tromped into my shoebox and made herself at home. Her hair was truly spectacular. It looked like she might have even pulled out a clump on the left side. "You want to tell me why the sheriff and alpha of Hung Island, Georgia says he won't work with you?"

"Um…no?"

"He said he had a hard time believing someone as flaky and irresponsible as you had become an agent for the Council and he wants someone else." Angela narrowed her eyes at me and took the remote form Dwayne. "Spill it, Essie."

I figured the best way to handle this was to lie— hugely. However, gay Vampyre boyfriends had a way of interrupting and screwing up all your plans.

"Well, you see…"

"He's her mate and he dipped his stick in several other…actually *many* other oil tanks. So she dumped his furry player ass, snuck away in the middle of the night and hadn't really planned on ever going back there again." Dwayne sucked in a huge breath, which was ridiculous because Vampyres didn't breathe.

It took everything I had not to scream and go all Wolfy. "Dwayne, clearly you want me to go medieval on your lily white ass because I can't imagine why you would utter such bullshit to my boss."

"Doesn't sound like bullshit to me," Angela said as she channel surfed and landed happily on an old episode of *Cagney and Lacey*. "We might have a problem here."

"Are you replacing me?" Hank Wilson had screwed me over once when I was his. He was not going to do it again when I wasn't.

"Your call," she said. Dwayne, who was an outstanding shoplifter, covertly took back the remote and flipped over to the Food Channel. Angela glanced up at the tube and gave Dwayne the evil eye.

"I refuse to watch lesbians fight crime in the eighties. I'll get hives," he explained, tilted his head to the right and gave Angela a smile. He was so pretty it was silly—piercing blue eyes and body to die for. Even my boss had a hard time resisting his charm.

"Fine," she grumbled.

"Excuse me," I yelled. "This conversation is about me, not testosterone ridden women cops with bad hair, hives or food. It's my life we're talking about here—me, me, me!" My voice had risen to decibels meant to attract stray animals within a ten-mile radius, evidenced by the wincing and ear covering.

"Essie, are you done?" Dwayne asked fearfully.

"Possibly. What did you tell him?" I asked Angela.

"I told him the Council has the last word in all matters. Always. And if he had a problem with it, he could take it up with the elders next month when they stay awake long enough to listen to the petitions of their people."

"Oh my god, that's awesome," I squealed. "What did he say?"

"That if we send you down, he'll give you bus money so you can hightail your sorry cowardly butt right back out of town."

Was she grinning at me, and was that little shit Dwayne jotting the conversation down in the notes section on his phone?

"Let me tell you something," I ground out between clenched teeth as I confiscated Dwayne's phone and pocketed it. "I am going to Hung Island, Georgia tomorrow and I will kick his ass. I will find the killer first and then I will castrate the alpha of the Georgia Pack...with a dull butter knife."

Angela laughed and Dwayne jackknifed over on the couch in a visceral reaction to my plan. I stomped into my bathroom and slammed the door to make my point, then pressed my ear to the rickety wood to hear them talk behind my back.

"I'll bet you five hundred dollars she's gonna bang him," Dwayne told Angela.

"I'll bet you a thousand that you're right," she shot back.

"You're on."

CHAPTER 2

"This music is going to make me yack." Dwayne moaned and put his hands over his ears.

Trying to ignore him wasn't working. I promised myself I wouldn't put him out of the car until we were at least a hundred miles outside of Chicago. I figured anything less than that wouldn't be the kind of walk home that would teach him a lesson.

"First of all, Vampyres can't yack and I don't recall asking you to come with me," I replied and cranked up The Clash.

"You have got to be kidding." He huffed and flipped the station to Top Forty. "You need me."

"Really?"

"Oh my god," Dwayne shrieked. "I luurrve Lady Gaga."

"That's why I need you?"

"Wait. What?"

"I need you because you love The Gaga?"

Dwayne rolled his eyes. "Everyone loves The Gaga. You need me because you need to show your hometown and Hank the Hooker that you have a new man in your life."

"You're a Vampyre."

"Yes, and?"

"Well, um...you're gay."

"What does that have to do with anything? I am hotter than asphalt in August and I have a huge package."

While his points were accurate, there was no mistaking his sexual preference. The skinny jeans, starched muscle shirt, canvas Mary Janes and the gold hoop earrings were an undead giveaway.

"You know, I think you should just be my best friend. I want to show them I don't need a man to make it in this world...okay?" I glanced over and he was crying. Shitshitshit. Why did I always say the wrong thing? "Dwayne, I'm sorry. You can totally be my..."

"You really consider me your best friend?" he blubbered. "I have never had a best friend in all my three hundred years. I've tried, but I just..." He broke down and let her rip.

"Yes, you're my best friend, you idiot. Stop crying. Now." Snark I could deal with. Tears? Not so much.

"Oh my god, I just feel so happy," he gushed. "And I want you to know if you change your mind about the boyfriend thing just wink at me four times and I'll stick my tongue down your throat."

"Thanks, I'll keep that in mind."

"Anything for my best friend. Ohhh Essie, are there any gay bars in Hung?"

This was going to be a wonderful trip.

***

One way in to Hung Island, Georgia. One way out. The bridge was long and the ocean was beautiful. Sun glistened off the water and sparkled like diamonds. Dwayne was quiet for the first time in fifteen hours. As we

185

pulled into town, my gut clenched and I started to sweat. This was stupid—so very stupid. The nostalgic pull of this place was huge and I felt sucked back in immediately.

"Holy Hell," Dwayne whispered. "It's beautiful here. How did you leave this place?"

He was right. It was beautiful. It had the small town feel mixed up with the ocean and land full of wild grasses and rolling hills. How did I leave?

"I left because I hate it here," I lied. "We'll do the job, castrate the alpha with a butter knife and get out. You got it?"

"Whatever you say, best friend. Whatever you say." He grinned.

"I'm gonna drop you off at my Grandma Bobby Sue's. She doesn't exactly know we're coming so you have to be on your best behavior."

"Will you be?"

"Will I be what?" God, Vamps were tiresome.

"On your best behavior."

"Absolutely not. We're here."

I stopped my crappy car in front of a charming old Craftsman. Flowers covered every inch of the yard. It was a literal explosion of riotous color and I loved it. Granny hated grass—found the color offensive. It was the home I grew up in. Granny BS, as everyone loved to call her, had raised me after my parents died in a horrific car accident when I was four. I barely remembered my parents, but Granny had told me beautiful bedtime stories about them my entire childhood.

"OMG, this place is so cute I could scream." Dwayne squealed and jumped out of the car into the blazing sunlight. All the stories about Vamps burning to ash or sparkling like diamonds in the sun were a myth. The only thing that could kill Weres and Vamps were silver bullets, decapitation, fire and a silver stake in the heart.

Grabbing Dwayne by the neck of his muscle shirt, I stopped him before he went tearing into the house. "Granny is old school. She thinks Vamps are...you know."

"Blood sucking leeches who should be eliminated?" Dwayne grinned from ear to ear. He loved a challenge. Crap.

"I wouldn't go that far, but she's old and set in her geezer ways. So if you have to, steer clear."

"I'll have her eating kibble out of my manicured lily white hand in no time at...holy shit!" Dwayne screamed and ducked as a blur of Granny BS came flying out of the house and tackled my ass in a bed of posies.

"Mother Humper." I grunted and struggled as I tried to shove all ninety-five pounds of pissed off Grandma Werewolf away from me.

"Gimme that stomach," she hissed as she yanked up my shirt. Thank the Lord I was wearing a bra. Dwayne stood in mute shock and just watched me get my butt handed to me by my tiny granny, who even at eighty was the spitting image of a miniature Sophia Loren in her younger years.

"Get off of me, you crazy old bag," I ground out and tried to nail her with a solid left. She ducked and backslapped my head.

"I said no tattoos and no piercings till you're fifty," she yelled. "Where is it?"

"Oh my GOD," I screeched as I trapped her head with my legs in a scissors hold. "You need meds."

"Tried 'em. They didn't work," she grumbled as she escaped from my hold. She grabbed me from behind as I tried to make a run for my car and ripped out my belly button ring.

"Ahhhhhhgrhupcraaap, that hurt, you nasty old bat from Hell." I screamed and looked down at the bloody hole that used to be really cute and sparkly. "That was a one carat diamond, you ancient witch."

Both of her eyebrows shot up and I swear to god they touched her hairline.

"Okay, fine," I muttered. "It was cubic zirconia, but it was NOT cheap."

"Hookers have belly rings," she snapped.

"No, hookers have pimps. Normal people have belly rings, or at least they used to," I shot back as I examined the wound that was already closing up.

"Come give your granny a hug," she said and put her arms out.

I approached warily just in case she needed to dole out more punishment for my piercing transgression. She folded me into her arms and hugged me hard. That was the thing about my granny. What you saw was what you got. Everyone always knew where they stood with her. She was mad and then she was done. Period.

"Lawdy, I have missed you, child," she cooed.

"Missed you too, you old cow." I grinned and hugged her back. I caught Dwayne out of the corner of my eye. He was even paler than normal if that was possible and he had placed his hands over his pierced ears.

"Granny, I brought my…"

"Gay Vampyre best friend," she finished my introduction. She marched over to him, slapped her hands on her skinny hips and stared. She was easily a foot shorter than Dwayne, but he trembled like a baby. "Do you knit?" she asked him.

"Um…no, but I've always wanted to learn," he choked out.

188

She looked him up and down for a loooong minute, grunted and nodded her head. "We'll get along just fine then. Get your asses inside before the neighbors call the cops."

"Why would they call the cops?" Dwayne asked, still terrified.

"Well boy, I live amongst humans and I just walloped my granddaughter on the front lawn. Most people don't think that's exactly normal."

"Point," he agreed and hightailed it to the house.

"Besides," she cackled. "Wouldn't want the sheriff coming over to arrest you now, would we?"

I rolled my eyes and flipped her the bird behind her back.

"Saw that, girlie," she said.

Holy Hell, she still had eyes in the back of her head. If I was smart, I'd grab Dwayne, get in my car and head back to Chicago...but I had a killer to catch and a whole lot to prove here. Smart wasn't on my agenda today.

CHAPTER 3

The house was exactly the same as it was the last time I saw it a year ago. Granny had more crap on her tables, walls and shelves than an antique store. Dwayne was positively speechless and that was good. Granny took her décor seriously.

"I'm a little disappointed that you want to be a model, Essie," Granny sighed. "You have brains and a mean right hook. Never thought you'd try to coast by with your looks."

I gave Dwayne the *I'll kill you if you tell her I'm an agent on a mission* look and thankfully he understood. While I hated that my granny thought I was shallow and jobless, it was far safer that she didn't know why I was really here.

"Well, you know…I just need to make a few bucks, then get back to my life in the big city," I mumbled. I was a sucky liar around my granny and she knew it.

"Hmmm," she said, staring daggers at me.

"What?" I asked, not exactly making eye contact.

"Nothin'. I'm just lookin'," she challenged.

"And what are you looking at?" I blew out an exasperated sigh and met her eyes. A challenge was a challenge and I *was* a Werewolf…

"A bald face little fibber girl," she crowed. "Spill it or I'll whoop your butt again."

Dwayne quickly backed himself into a corner and slid his phone out of his pocket. That shit was going to video my ass kicking. I had several choices here...destroy Dwayne's phone, elaborate on my lie or come clean. The only good option was the phone.

"Fine," I snapped and sucked in a huge breath. The truth will set you free or result in a trip to the ER... "I'm an agent with the Council—a trained killer for WTF and I'm good at it. The fact that I'm a magnet for trouble has finally paid off. I'm down here to find out who in the hell is killing Werewolves before it blows up in our faces. I plan to find the perps and destroy them with my own hands or a gun, whichever will be most painful. Then I'm going to castrate Hank with a dull butter knife. I plan on a short vacation when I'm done before going back to Chicago."

For the first time in my twenty-eight years on Earth, Granny was mute. It was all kinds of awesome.

"Can I come on the vacation?" Dwayne asked.

"Yes. Cat got your tongue, old woman?" I asked.

"Well, I'll be damned," she said almost inaudibly. "I suppose this shouldn't surprise me. You are a female alpha bitch."

"No," I corrected her. "I'm a lone wolf who wants nothing to do with Pack politics. Ever."

Granny sat her skinny bottom down on her plastic slipcovered floral couch and shook her head. "Ever is a long time, little girl. Well, I suppose I should tell you something now," she said gravely and worried her bottom lip.

"Oh my god, are you sick?" I gasped. Introspective thought was way out of my granny's normal behavior pattern. My stomach roiled. She was all I had left in the world and as much as I wanted to skin her alive, I loved her even more.

"Weres don't get sick. It's about your mamma and daddy. Sit down. And Dwayne, hand over your phone. If I find out you have loose lips, I'll remove them," she told my bestie.

I sat. Dwayne handed. I had thought I knew everything there was to know about my parents, but clearly I was mistaken. Hugely mistaken.

"You remember when I told you your mamma and daddy died in a car accident?"

"Yes," I replied slowly. "You showed me the newspaper articles."

"That's right." She nodded. "They did die in a car, but it wasn't no accident."

Movement was necessary or I thought I might throw up. I paced the room and tried to untangle my thoughts. It wasn't like I'd even known my parents, but they were mine and now I felt cheated somehow. I wanted to crawl out of my skin. My heart pounded so loudly in my chest I was sure the neighbors could hear it. My parents were murdered and this was the first time I was hearing about it?

"Again. Say that again." Surely I'd misunderstood. I'd always been one to jump to conclusions my entire life, but the look on Granny's face told me that this wasn't one of those times.

"They didn't own a hardware store. Well, actually I think they did, but it was just a cover."

"For what?" I asked, fairly sure I knew where this was going.

"They were WTF agents, child, and they were taken out," she said and wrapped her skinny little arms around herself. "Broke my heart—still does."

"And you never told me this? Why?" I demanded and got right up in her face.

"I don't rightly know," she said quietly. "I wanted you to grow up happy and not feel the need for revenge."

She stroked my cheek the way she did when I was a child and I leaned into her hand for comfort. I was angry, but she did what she thought was right. Needless to say, she wasn't right, but...

"Wait, why would I have felt the need for revenge?" I asked. Something was missing.

"The Council was never able to find out who did it, and after a while they gave up."

Everything about that statement was so wrong I didn't know how to react. They gave up? What the hell was that? The Council never gave up. I was trained to get to the bottom of everything. Always.

"That's the most absurd thing I've ever heard. The Council always gets their answers."

Granny shrugged her thin shoulders and rearranged the knickknacks on her coffee table. Wait. Did the Council know more about me than I did? Did my boss Angela know more of my history than I'd ever known?

"I knew that recruiter they sent down here," Granny muttered. "I told him to stay away from you. Told him the Council already took my daughter and son-in-law and they couldn't have you."

"He didn't pay me any more attention than he did anyone else," I told her.

"What did the flyer say that he gave you?"

"Same as everybody's—salary, training, benefits, car, apartment."

"Damn it to hell," she shouted. "No one else's flyer said that. I confiscated them all after the bastard left. I couldn't get to yours cause you were shacking up with the sheriff."

"You lived with Hank the Hooker?" Dwayne gasped. "I thought you just dated a little."

"Hell to the no," Granny corrected Dwayne. "She was engaged. Left the alpha of the Georgia Pack high and dry."

"Enough," I snapped. "Ancient history. I'm more concerned about what kind of cow patty I've stepped in with the Council. The *sheriff* knows why I left. Maybe the Council accepted me cause I can shoot stuff and I have no fear and they have to hire a certain quota of women and..."

"And they want to make sure you don't dig into the past," Dwayne added unhelpfully.

"You're a smart bloodsucker," Granny chimed in.

"Thank you."

"You think the Council had something to do with it," I said. This screwed with my chi almost as much as the Hank situation from a year ago. I had finally done something on my own and it might turn out I hadn't earned any of it.

"I'm not sayin' nothing like that," Granny admonished harshly. "And neither should you. You could get killed."

She was partially correct, but I was the one they sent to kill people who broke Council laws. However, speaking against the Council wasn't breaking the law. The living room had grown too small for my need to move and I prowled the rest of the house with Granny and Dwayne on my heels. I stopped short and gaped at my empty bedroom.

"Where in the hell is my furniture?"

"You moved all your stuff to Hank's and he won't give it back," Granny informed me.

An intense thrill shot through my body, but I tamped it down immediately. I was done with him and he was surely done with me. No one humiliated an alpha and got a second chance. Besides, I didn't want one... Dwayne's snicker earned him a glare that made him hide behind Granny in fear.

"Did you even try to get my stuff back?" I demanded.

"Of course I did," she huffed. "That was your mamma's set from when she was a child. I expected you'd use it for your own daughter someday."

My mamma...My beautiful mamma who'd been murdered along with my daddy. The possibility that the Council had been involved was gnawing at my insides in a bad way.

"I have to compartmentalize this for a minute or at least a couple of weeks," I said as I stood in the middle of my empty bedroom. "I have to do what I was sent here for. But when I'm done, I'll get answers and vengeance."

"Does that mean no vacation?" Dwayne asked.

I stared at Dwayne like he'd grown three heads. He was getting terribly good at rendering me mute.

"That was a good question, Dwayne." Granny patted him on the head like a dog and he preened. "Essie, your mamma and daddy would want you to have a vacation before you get killed finding out what happened to them."

"Can we go to Jamaica?" Dwayne asked.

"Ohhh, I've never been to Jamaica," Granny volunteered.

They were both batshit crazy, but Jamaica did sound kind of nice...

"Fine, but you're paying," I told Dwayne. He was richer than Midas. He'd made outstanding investments in his three hundred years.

"Yayayayayayay!" he squealed.

195

"I'll call the travel agent," Granny said. "How long do you need to get the bad guy?"

"A week. Give me a week."

** Visit **www.robynpeterman.com** for more information.**

EXCERPT FROM ARIEL: NANO WOLVES 1

NANO WOLVES SERIES

BOOK DESCRIPTION

Being a living experiment wasn't part of the scientific career she'd planned for herself.

Despite her sharp scientific mind and her degree in bio-molecular genetics, Dr. Ariel Jones hasn't figured out how her life changed so much in a single day. Before she can blink and ask about what is going on, she is injected with a billion nanos and some very potent wolf blood.

Now she can suddenly turn into a giant white wolf with the bloodlust of a starving animal. And she's an alpha...or so she is told by the even larger, very male, black wolf who was used to create her. Hallucination? She wishes. Whether human or wolf, Reed talks in her head and tells her how to handle things... or rather how to kill them... starting with the men who hold them all captive. Too bad he can't tell her how to put her life back like it was.

Admittedly, there are perks to being a werewolf, such as meeting sexy werewolf guys like Matthew Gray Wolf. Science labs aren't overrun with sexy men in white coats. She also doesn't mind learning about a side of herself she never knew existed. It's great changing into a real wolf whenever she wants, but being a living experiment wasn't part of the scientific career she'd planned for herself. Neither was falling for the local werewolf alpha, but what else is a newbie werewolf caught in her burning time going to do?

CHAPTER 1

Dr. Ariel Jones blinked at the bright lights overhead as she woke. Finding herself naked and strapped to some sort of gurney, she turned her head and saw two women similarly strapped to gurneys beside her. One was weeping steadily. The other was glaring at a fixed spot on the ceiling.

Her scientist brain got busy immediately, trying to figure out what had happened since she'd come to work that morning. Her typical day at Feldspar Research always started at five in the morning to accommodate the light limitations of living and working just outside Anchorage, Alaska.

She had processed the new set of blood samples waiting for her in the lab and instantly reported the unusually rapid cell mutation she had seen happening under the lens of her microscope. Then at about ten o'clock, she'd gone for a direct meeting with Dr. Crane, who had asked to speak with her in person about what she'd found.

One minute she had been drinking coffee and talking with a colleague. The next she was waking up naked in...where was she anyway? Looking around more, she finally recognized the place. It was where they had brought the giant wolf.

Sniffing the air, she could indeed smell the pungency of the trapped animal. It was what had bothered her most. From what she knew, he'd been here longer than she had worked for Crane. The one and only time she'd seen the wolf in person had been more than enough. He was the biggest animal she'd ever seen and bigger than any she could have ever imagined.

Now she was here—in the same room where they had kept him. The discovery brought her back to her own pressing problem of waking up naked and restrained without knowing why. A thousand thoughts raced through her mind, none of them pleasant.

"So good of you to join us at last, Dr. Jones. I've been delaying things and waiting for you to wake up. I didn't want to start the injections while you were still under the effects of the mild sedative we gave you earlier."

"You put drugs in my coffee this morning," Ariel stated, somehow sure of it even before her bastard employer nodded and smiled.

"The sedative was the fastest way to obtain your physical cooperation. Time is critical. We don't know how long the window of opportunity from your findings will remain open. You told me several weeks ago you had come to Alaska because you craved more out of life than sitting in a lab doing research. Well, I'm about to make your dreams come true in a way you have never imagined."

Ignoring her accelerating heartbeat, Ariel decided she wasn't going to get emotionally alarmed until there was a greater reason to do so than simply being naked and unable to free herself. She was used to thinking her way out of bad situations. She just needed to remain calm, ask questions, and figure out what was really going on.

"I would like to know the purpose of your actions. Are you planning to take physical advantage of my helpless condition? Who are the two women next to me? What role do they play?"

Dr. Crane smiled. "So many questions. Of course, I expected someone like you would have them. You're going on a scientific adventure or at least your body is. The three of you are about to become the next step in the evolution of our species. But I guess it's rather bold of me to theorize such a result without any proof yet. Part of the excitement is considering all the possibilities. Now I know your circumstances are a bit alarming at the moment, but if this experiment works, you'll become an extremely valuable asset to our military. Even the most highly trained K-9 units won't be able to compete with your animal skills. Alaskan wolves are quite superior to canines in nearly all areas. Everyone studies their predatory actions for just this reason."

"I still don't understand, Dr. Crane. I thought Feldspar was testing wolf fortitude to glean survival information for living in extremely harsh environments," Ariel said, discreetly testing the restraints around her wrists again.

"Oh come now, Dr. Jones. That sort of work is barely fit for a second year university student. You are here because you personally possess several strands of DNA in common with our latest Feldspar wolf acquisition. He's been rather solemn since we informed him of your findings. He's glaring at us steadily which I take as the highest compliment about your discovery. It's as if he senses what we are about to do to the three of you."

"Dr. Crane, are you saying you're communicating with a wolf? Don't you think that assumption is a bit odd?" Ariel asked.

"Not at all. I sincerely wish we could be communicating with his human side, but we've purposely kept him from shifting back to his human form by the silver collar around his neck. I think it helped greatly to leave the six silver bullets someone put into him too. He was initially impossible to capture in his wolf form. If his pack had been nearby, I doubt we would have. In fact, I don't know who exactly did capture him. I found him both shot and tranquilized with a note pinned to his collar when someone activated the alarm on the back door of the lab."

"I'm sorry Dr. Crane, but you sound like some crazy mad scientist out of a movie. What are you going to do to us? Seriously? You don't have to make up such wild stories. I assure you I won't be reduced to hysterics by hearing the truth," Ariel demanded.

"Still the skeptical scientist, I see. In just a moment, I'll happily explain the rest to you. Since what's going to happen to you is beyond your control, I don't see any benefit from not telling you the whole story." Dr. Crane waved at the man assisting him. "Proceed with injecting the weeping one on the end. I cannot tolerate a weeping female. She is highly distracting. I can't talk to Dr. Jones over her constant whining."

Ariel's head whipped over, straining to see the gurney at the end. She saw the woman's body arch when a plunger was placed at her neck directly on the carotid artery. Whatever was in the injection, they wanted it to hit all parts of her body quickly. To her surprise, the man rolled the woman's head, and shot a second plunger directly into the woman's brain stem. The woman seized, strained at her straps, and then fell silent. If the second injection didn't paralyze her spine, its content would be in every brain cell in less than ten minutes.

"Now administer the sedative and move Heidi to the last cage. Come straight back and process Brandi next. I'll take care of Dr. Jones personally."

Ariel looked back at the man speaking so calmly. He looked at her and offered a shrug.

"The sedative is to help keep you calm during the worst of your genetic transmutation. We're not completely without conscience. I see no need for any of you to suffer more than necessary. Since you're the first of your kind, we don't exactly know how much the transpecies mutation process hurts. Our captive wolf shifter has been quite unwilling to share any information, assuming he can still speak in his wolf form. We haven't been able to ascertain it one way or the other."

The woman directly beside her was still as quiet as ever. So far, she had not made a sound. Ariel listened to the gurney with the now unconscious Heidi being pushed to the far end of the room. She listened to a cage door being opened and straps being undone.

"Please continue your explanation, Dr. Crane. Did I find something important this morning?"

"Yes, you did. I applaud you for being as smart as your resume indicated. People usually lie on those you know. Somehow I knew right away when we met that you were being honest. It was quite the stroke of luck your blood also showed excellent—most excellent—counts of nearly everything required for the experiment. When I personally saw the metamorphosis strand in your DNA, I was literally as giddy as a schoolboy. The strand is missing from your fellow subjects."

"I did my doctoral thesis on the metamorphosis strand. Most in the scientific community don't even think its real. But I've seen it. People who have it tend to die fairly young. It's one of the reasons I left New England and came here. I wanted to explore the world a little before I came down with some disease I couldn't survive."

"Yes. Human subjects with the strand do tend to die young. But extending your doctoral hypothesis, I also believe the strand has a higher purpose in those who possess it. So when I saw from the extensive health exams Feldspar required that you personally had the strand, I just couldn't pass up the opportunity. Roger, I said to myself, what would happen if someone extremely intelligent suddenly became a wild animal? Would the person be able to control their carnal nature enough to use their intelligence in their animal form? The chance to discover the truth was just too much to pass up. Now you get to benefit from the very discovery you made this morning, Dr. Jones. It's too bad the global medical community will never know anything more about you except for the unfortunate accident which burnt your body to ashes today when you went into Anchorage for lunch. Alaskan winters can be terribly challenging on vehicles, as I'm sure your gurney mates can also attest to since they suffered the same fate."

Ariel flinched when she heard the woman beside her hiss and swear at the depression of the plunger at her neck. When her brain stem was shot, the woman shrieked loudly and nearly broke the straps with her arching. The sedative calmed the woman instantly, but it had the opposite effect on Ariel. Starting to panic at last, because she knew the same fate would be hers, Ariel renewed her efforts to escape and twisted against her restraints. Unfortunately, she lacked the strength to break them.

She listened to the second gurney being wheeled down the hall. Again a cage door opened. Moments later, she heard it close and a key turning in a lock.

"Who gave you the right to do this to us, Dr. Crane? I came to Feldspar to do research for you, not to *be* your research. What you are doing is illegal and immoral."

"I know. I do feel a little bad about hiring you under false pretenses, but your discovery this morning stacked the odds in favor of your participation. My benefactor is most anxious to see some evidence that the transpecies mutation process can work. If even one of you survives the change, he will fund me for at least another two years."

"You're the sickest, sorriest excuse for a scientist I've ever met," Ariel declared.

Dr. Crane nodded as he lifted the first injection into the air above her. "Not anymore. Now I'm the scientist who has figured out how to make werewolves. As far as I know, I'm the only one like me on Earth. My services will be highly sought after when I show them a brilliant scientist in her wolf form."

Ariel called out and felt fire crawl under her skin as sizzling hot liquid entered her bloodstream. *"Nanos?* You injected me with nanos? It feels like a billion ants crawling on the inside of my skin." She saw Crane lift an eyebrow at her knowledge, but then so did she. She wasn't even sure how she knew what they were giving her.

"You're very sharp, Dr. Jones, much too sharp to spend your life doing research. I picked women as initial test subjects because they could be physically restrained the easiest. I did not plan on using a woman who would be able to figure out what was going on. But that's what makes life interesting. Now the next injection has to go directly into the brain steam for best results. I'm sorry for the extreme pain it causes. Judging from your fellow test subjects, the pain won't last more than a few moments."

Ariel fought as the assistant turned her head and held it still while Dr. Crane positioned the plunger. The depression happened quickly. Pain more intense than anything she'd ever known shot through her head and had her calling out. Before her consciousness faded, her last thought was that Dr. Crane had lied to her. She had been spared nothing. Her head exploding from the inside was what dropped the eventual black veil over her thoughts.

She never felt the sedative working at all.

CHAPTER 2

Ariel shook with cold as she came up out of a deep, drugged sleep. Naked and shivering, she determined that she was lying on a small cot.

As she struggled to open her eyes, she could just barely make out the forms of Dr. Crane and his white-coated asswipe of an assistant. They were staring into the cages where they'd stashed the other two women who had been captured alongside her. There was a bunch of growling and hissing which kept getting louder as the men talked.

Dr. Crane looked extremely pleased with whatever was happening. The knowledge pissed her off, but her dark thoughts of doing vicious and hideously cruel things to both men surprised her.

Ariel lifted a pale hand in front of her face, which blurred out of focus, but finally came back in. So far, nothing overly unusual had happened to her body, unless you counted the sick headache she had at the moment. She felt strange though—very strange. Her stomach growled with fierce hunger and there was a steady fire burning between her legs. Those two white-coated bastards had better not have touched her. If they did, she was cutting off their man parts and throwing them in the recycler. Later, when she was more alert, she promised herself she would check her body closer.

A loud clanging against the bars of her cage had her covering her ears. Sound—all sound—hurt terribly and increased her headache. A percussion band played in her head as she fought the pain.

"I'm afraid your doctoral thesis is now a complete failure, Dr. Jones. Apparently, the metamorphosis strand is a deterrent to transpecies mutation as well as being something to shorten a person's life. Now I have to decide what to do about you. We can't just turn you loose in society and have you telling everyone what we're up to here. You were certainly a waste of a couple billion very expensive nanos we can't get back. Sadly, you've become the only failure case, rather than the pinnacle of our success."

It took her a lot of effort, but Ariel finally managed to manipulate her hand enough to get her middle finger to stand up alone. Crane's laugh at her silent rebellion grated on every nerve she had, not to mention how much his voice hurt her ears.

"When I get out of here, I may kill you just to watch you hurt," Ariel croaked, her mouth dry as dust.

Crane laughed harder and walked away. At his departure, the growling and hissing in the cages next to her ceased. When the room was totally silent once more, she drifted back into a peaceful oblivion where she could pretend nothing had happened.

***

Dr. Jones—Ariel. Wake now, but do not shift. Wake in human form. Think of yourself as human and you will be one.

Ariel rolled to her side on the canvas cot and tried to pull the scratchy cover she'd found over her naked body. Even with her knees scrunched up, it was far too short. She covered her eyes with a hand as she fought off the nightmares which were now continuously talking to her. There must have been hallucinogens in what they gave her.

I am not a hallucination. I am Reed—a three hundred year old alpha. You are a two day old version. It is very wise of your wolf to hide itself from those who seek to harm you.

Ariel groaned and rolled to the other side. "Head hurts. Stop talking to me."

I know you are in pain, but you must fight off the drugs now. Crane returns soon. He is planning to move you to another facility and dissect your body to find out why conversion failed with you. They have identified another experiment victim and she arrives tomorrow. You must rescue the others and kill Crane before he can turn more.

"Kill Crane? Sure. I'd love to do that," she repeated, covering her eyes with her hands.

Yes. I regret the extremeness of the step, but Roger Crane must not be allowed to continue his work. You will have to destroy the lab as well. Accidents happen all the time in Alaska. I doubt Feldspar Research will fund any other scientist if we completely destroy the proof of Crane's success.

"O—K." she said groggily, working her body into an upright position. Sitting up hurt as much as anything else did. "And I thought my divorce was traumatic. Either my nightmares are getting bossy or I'm hearing real voices in my head."

Putting a hand up to her head, she rubbed the base of her skull where they had shot something into her brain stem.

"Hey nightmare, since we're on a speaking basis, do you know what the hell Crazy Crane shot me with in the back of my head?"

My blood—I believe. He took it at the pinnacle of my wolf's lunar cycle. Since I was already in my wolf form when he caught me, hitting the lunar pinnacle was evidently strong enough to cause a species turning. I had heard the legends, but human turnings have not been done since the middle ages. Packs prefer to propagate organically. Unfortunately, Crane found a way to take the choice from me.

Ariel laughed. Her intuition spoke to her all the time, but it usually didn't announce she was a wolf in human form. "Hey Nightmare, are we going to keep talking in my head?"

Yes. I am your alpha. You are an alpha in training. So yes — we will talk in your head — until we can do so differently. I cannot shift from my wolf until the bullets and collar are removed from me. Silver has a restraining effect.

"Being shot with your blood doesn't make you my dad or anything, does it?" Ariel could have swore her nightmare wolf tried to laugh. He huffed like a dog doing it.

No. But it does make you my responsibility until you take a mate who can look out for you. Being part of a pack is like having a large family. I think you might like it once you understand it.

Ariel snorted. "So I'm an alpha. Does being alpha mean you're top dog or something?"

We are canis lupis, not dogs. Alaska is home to more than eleven thousand wolves. More than half are what humans call werewolves. This is what you have become, Ariel Jones. You are now both human and wolf, as are the other two females. They are your charges and the first of your pack. They are your responsibility and will look to you for guidance on how to adjust to their new lives.

His comments—which she was starting to believe weren't just voices in her head—had Ariel standing on wobbly legs and walking to the bars of her prison. In the cages next to hers, two multi-colored wolves paced restlessly. They were less than half the size of the black wolf, but still real enough to convince her she wasn't just having a nightmare. Oh no—she was living one.

"Brandi. Heidi. Relax. We're going to escape. I promise." When both multi-colored wolves sat and turned to her expectantly, Ariel shook her head. She knew their names and could command their obedience. Though she'd never been a person given to swearing, there were no normal words to express the enormity of her shock. Was she truly going to one day be a wolf as well?

"Un—fucking—believable," she whispered. She turned her head until she saw the edge of the giant black wolf as he leaned against one side of his cage. "Reed? Is the giant black wolf you?"

Yes, Ariel. The giant black wolf is me. You should see the alpha of the Wasilla Pack. Matt's wolf is even bigger.

She felt like peeing herself when the black wolf turned his head and met her gaze like a human would during a conversation. He had the greenest eyes she'd ever seen on a man or animal. They were filled with a kind of determination she'd never felt before, but had a feeling she was about to get an education in it.

Crane returns. I know it is him. His stench will haunt me for the next hundred years of my life.

"Okay. I'm wide awake now and mostly willing to believe you," she said, hoping all three wolves understood she was working her way to acceptance as fast as she could. She went back to her cot and huddled under the short cover. "Hey Reed, did I get bigger or something?"

Yes. And you are strong enough to kill the men who will be trying to kill you. You have to try, Ariel. It is important to me that you and the other women survive. When they open the cage to take you out of it, call your wolf to help. She will be more than happy to answer. I've been helping you hold her back until the time was right.

"My mind is having a hell of a time trying to believe all of this is real, but I'm sure as hell not ready to die. Let's say I believe you. What does my wolf look like?"

Until she comes, none of us will know. I just hope she's big and strong. Rest now and pretend to be weak. You do not want them to know what you really are until it is too late.

210

Ariel leaned back on the cot and tried to look as pathetic as possible so her captors would believe she was just as harmless as they assumed she was.

Inside, she was praying that Reed—or whatever inner voice was helping her survive—was right about her being able to free them all.

CHAPTER 3

Despite the fact Reed had said he smelled Crane, it was almost a half hour before the two men finally came back into the room. Assistant asswipe walked to her cage immediately and unlocked the door without a thought. He came in and grabbed her arm, forcefully lifting her to her feet. She jerked away from his hold and walked to the door of the cage on her own, staring at Dr. Crane, who was standing just outside, waiting on her exit. Two steps later and she was free of her prison. Something inside her seemed to expand in relief.

"What you did to me sort of negates saying you're the worst employer I've ever had, Dr. Crane. So instead of saying I quit, I'm going to say I'm done being your science experiment."

When both his eyebrows rose at her firm statement, Ariel dropped the insufficient blanket and stood in front of him completely nude. She heard asswipe chuckling behind her. She could smell their lack of concern and hear it in their steady heartbeats. Something in her rejoiced in the knowledge. Their complacency was going to be their downfall.

Assistant Asswipe suddenly smacked her bare ass and made her yelp in surprise. Crane laughed at his goon's actions, but didn't chastise him for it.

Fire suddenly raced through her unchecked. She felt the nanos scrambling under her skin. In a blink, she was on all fours and leaping on Assistant Asswipe. One minute he was screaming in shock and the next he was silent because it was impossible to talk with your throat ripped out. She wasn't even tempted to eat the man, no matter how much she was starving. Turning loose finally, she turned to Crane who was walking backwards to the lab door.

"Look at you, Dr. Jones. You're absolutely magnificent. To think all this time, you were a giant golden wolf. And almost as large as the acquisition. How were you able to fight off the change for so long?"

Ariel heard him talking, but his words meant nothing. She leapt into the air toward the bastard who had tormented her, only to feel a taser hook attach to her chest while she was still several feet away. She hit the lab floor with a thud, whimpering in pain as Crane sent voltage into her. She struggled at the end of the attached wire.

Writhing, she watched Crane walk to the wall and pull a silver collar off a peg. Ariel blinked her new eyes and recognized it was a match for the one Reed wore. She couldn't let Crane put the collar on her. She couldn't fail them all by letting Crane control her wolf.

Behind her, she heard Brandi and Heidi whimpering, but also growling and snarling.

I know it hurts, but you must fight for us, Ariel. You've killed one. Kill the other and free us all.

At hearing Reed's encouragement in her head, she rolled to a half-sitting position, lifting what felt like massive wolf's shoulders from the ground. It took a lot of effort. Crane sent another shock into her as he reached out with the open collar. Though it hurt to move, she lifted a giant paw and knocked the metal from his hand. He pressed the button on the taser, only to find it was out of juice. Her wolf quivered in relief.

A low growl started in her chest as Crane set the taser aside, casually rose, and headed to the door. He was definitely not leaving, not if she could stop him. She wobbled as she stood and took a couple unsteady steps. Crane's hand was on the access pad. She listened to him enter the exit code. Three – eight – nine – two. Maybe she was going to like having ears that could hear this well.

She braced herself and leapt on the back of him, dragging him to the floor by his white lab coat. He yelled once as she landed heavily on his back, but stopped struggling when she chomped on the back of his neck. She bit down until she felt something crack at the same time she punctured his jugular. Hot blood rushed into her mouth. Mad still, she raised up his body with her bite, which she soon realized covered his whole neck. She shook him back and forth even though the dead man was already totally limp.

Knowing she had indeed stopped Crane was the most amazing feeling. She walked around with the scientist clutched in her teeth, even trotting back to show Brandi and Heidi. They laid down on the floor and put their noses on their paws. Her pride over his death filled her with enormous satisfaction. The crazy scientist would never torture another female.

Enough, child. Let the dead man go. Don't contaminate your body by chewing on him. You need to change back to human form now and free us.

Whimpering, Ariel walked back and dropped Crane's body in front of Reed's cage. Part of her didn't want the cruel bastard to be dead yet. She wanted him to suffer longer—suffer the way she and the women had—the way Reed had. Maybe she shouldn't have bitten so hard. Maybe she should have done it in a way where he would have bled out and died slowly.

Ariel sat on her rear haunches and glared at the black wolf. How was she supposed to become human again? She didn't want to be human. She was happy in her wolf form.

Look at what she'd done. Her head turned and she whimpered again at the body of the man who had smacked her naked ass. She dropped her head to look at the other dead man in front of her.

If you change back, the others will follow your lead. You need human hands to unlock my cage...and theirs. You need human hands to gather up the evidence of Crane's experiments. Dr. Jones, I'm begging you to do this. You can be a wolf anytime you want now. I promise.

Her ears perked up. Dr. Jones? Yes. She had always liked being called that. Lying down, she laid her head on her paws and thought about becoming a female again. Fire consumed her once more, but not as much as it had when she had become her wolf. Again she felt the nanos getting busy under her skin.

A tortured groan split the air when she turned and saw a bloody Crane lying next to her, his dead eyes wide with shock.

"Shit. Did I really do that to him?"

Ariel raised to her knees gingerly and stared back at the cages.

"Did I really kill both of them?"

She looked back at Reed. He blinked, but said nothing to her, not even in her head. Of course she had killed them both. The memory of their deaths lived in her brain now. She had been a wolf, but she had been herself too. She just hadn't cared about anything but stopping them. She had no regrets.

When she could stand, she stumbled to Assistant Asswipe and fished the cage keys out of the pocket of his bloody lab coat. She looked at the wolves prowling the cages again. "Think of the women you were and change back. If you do that, I'll let you out."

Brandi laid down immediately and two seconds later, she was her normal self. Heidi still paced and whimpered, reluctant to do what they'd done. Ariel walked to the cage and stared at her. "Yes, it hurts, but it's necessary. Now do it, so we can get the hell out of here."

Whimpering harder than ever, Heidi laid down and moments later screeched as her human form took over. Ariel unlocked both cages as quickly as she could.

"In a minute, I'm going to set off the fire alarm. While that's distracting the building guard, go find us some long lab coats," she ordered. "There are two techs somewhere in the building who are going to stare at you both if they see you naked. They're harmless. Wiggle your fingers and giggle. They'll think you're the party girls Crane orders for entertainment on Fridays."

Brandi glared at her for her comments, but Heidi just hung her head. Apparently, one of them was a party girl. Ariel rolled her eyes at the knowledge and headed to unlock Reed's cage. He barely moved while she searched the key ring for the collar key. "I can't find it, Reed."

Leave me. Find Matt. He'll take care of you.

"No. I'm not leaving you. I'd be dead if it wasn't for you. You told me to save all of us and that's what I'm going to do."

Ariel left the cage open. She bent over Crane's body and ripped a wide swatch of fabric from the back of his blood soaked lab coat. She brought the fabric swatch back and wrapped it around the chain where it attached to the wall. She could feel the metal heat her skin as she tugged on it to test.

"Come on nanos. Get your little fixing asses to work. I've got to do this no matter how bad it hurts." She yanked and tugged and yanked some more. At this rate, it was going to take awhile.

Brandi appeared at her shoulder and without speaking took hold of the chain too. Ariel nodded at her stare. Breasts swinging with every yank, she and Brandi

216

pulled twice and then the damn thing popped free of the wall.

Ariel kept her fingers wrapped around the chain. Even through the fabric it was burning her skin. Not being able to handle silver had to be some kind of metal allergy. She was going to look into it sometime and see what the hell that was all about.

"Okay. You're free now. Let's go, Big Guy."

Reed stood, wavered, and then braced himself for each painful step. Ariel walked slowly as he limped out the door beside her. At the lab exit, Ariel deftly keyed in the code Crane had used earlier. The doors opened smoothly. She held it wide for the women who followed behind her and Reed.

Just outside the lab, Ariel rammed her fist into the door of a locked case in the wall, the glass cutting her knuckles. She ignored the pain which was already going away by the time the fire alarm filled the air. Her gut was overruling her brain. It was an odd sensation, but something urged her to trust it for the sake of all their lives.

"Go. Find us clothes. Do what I said," she ordered, turning to Brandi and Heidi. "Try to find us transportation too. Our vehicles are all dead. Crane drives a jeep. Let's take that. He's never going to need it again."

"Heidi, hold the door for me," Brandi ordered. She ran back into the lab and stooped to search Crane's pockets, brandishing jeep keys when she found them. Once she was outside the lab, Heidi closed the lab until the lock clicked.

Beside her, Ariel felt Heidi shiver. She turned and gave her a stern look. She had no time to deal with any emotional meltdowns. "Look—I don't know you and you don't know me. But I can tell you for certain that what was done to us can't be undone. All we can do is move forward. Unless you want to be responsible for Crane's backer coming after all of us, get your ass moving and follow Brandi out of here. We need to run while we can."

Both women nodded and ran off ahead. Heidi trailed behind Brandi only by a fraction.

The lab wasn't heavily staffed on Fridays. Knowing Crane, he'd made sure most of them weren't around for a few days during the experiment. She and Reed stopped at Crane's office. His laptop was open and still running on his desk. She took the time to turn off the screen lock before closing the lid and tucking it under one arm.

Next they stopped at her lab where she tugged on a lab coat she'd left there two days ago. She buttoned it up all the way to cover her nudity. Patting Reed on the head, she dropped his chain on the floor for a moment. "Wait here a minute."

Knowing she would heal fast because of the nanos, Ariel walked to the nearest chemical cabinet and repeated her bare knuckled fist pump through the glass. Reaching inside, she drew out the two most volatile chemicals it contained. Dumping both in a glass beaker she'd placed in a nearby sink, she watched the chemical reaction start to happen. She wanted to make sure it was working before they left.

"Come on, Reed. Compliments of my scientific education, that mix is going to have this room in flames in about five minutes. Then the whole building is going to go up when everything else in this lab explodes."

On the way out, she grabbed the largest microscope she could carry and tucked it under her arm. With Crane's laptop and a strong microscope, maybe she could start to unravel what had been done to them. Not that she believed she could ever reverse it. What she had said to Heidi still reverberated as truth. Nanos couldn't be removed once injected into you. They could be killed by extreme radiation, but never removed.

And Reed's blood was part of their molecular structure now. She wasn't sure how she knew that was a fact, but it felt like the same kind of truth as the nanos. Transpecies mutations weren't anything she'd learned in any genetics class. Knowledge of her blood connection to the black wolf who patiently waited for her came from sources she hadn't identified yet.

She picked up the silver chain still attached to Reed's collar, forgetting to wrap the cloth around it first. It burned like fire and stuck to her fingers, but there was no time left to think about the pain. Right now, they needed to vacate the premises before they went up in flames with it. By the time she and Reed got to the front door of the building, her hand was stinging like she'd rammed it into a hornet's nest. She was regretting her haste in leaving the fabric swatch behind.

When Brandi swerved in with the jeep two seconds later, Ariel and Reed both limped over to it. He made a running jump and nearly missed. Ariel caught his backside to push him up the rest of the way into the seat. He immediately curled up into a ball in the passenger's seat and shuddered. The effort to leave had obviously cost Reed the last of his energy. It made Ariel angry all over again. She turned a glare on the male who yelled at her.

"Why did you bust the wolf loose, Dr. Jones? You didn't seem the type. Are you one of those freaking animal lovers?" Feldspars' surly guard demanded.

Ariel glared briefly and then dismissed the speaker. The man and his attitude weren't important. Getting away was. "Yes, Frank. In this case, I am an animal lover. I'm setting the wolf free."

"Well, I hope you got everything you wanted when you got out, because you can't go back now anyway. You know this whole place is about to be blown all to hell, right?"

"Yes, I know, and good riddance," Ariel declared as she climbed into the backseat, plopping down beside Heidi. "Let's get out of here, Brandi."

Brandi shook her head, climbed out of the driver's side, and walked to the guard.

Before Ariel could figure out her intentions, Brandi grabbed and twisted the guard's head until she broke his neck. The man fell soundlessly to the ground. She watched Brandi drag him by one leg and throw him back into the building, closing the front door behind him. The lab techs were nowhere in sight. Ariel decided not knowing where they were was probably the best thing. She imagined they'd suffered the same fate as the irritating guard.

Fire engines were turning into the quarter mile long drive from the main road to the secluded facility as Brandi jogged back to the driver's seat. "The techs we talked to on the way are already headed home. I let them go because they were grieving your alleged death, but the guard recognized you, Dr. Jones. He was a loose end and would have given people way too much to talk about later if he had lived."

"Did you have to kill him? What if the man had a family?" Ariel demanded, biting her lip as Brandi swerved and drove down a side road she said would take them out a rarely used entrance.

"I don't think Frank had a family. He was too good a customer at the place where I worked," Heidi declared.

Ariel rolled her eyes. Seconds later a loud explosion rocked the air behind them. Black smoke filled the sky above a blazing Feldspar Research building.

Brandi kept driving calmly forward like buildings exploding around her happened every day. Ariel suddenly decided she wanted to know why—and why killing the guard hadn't caused her any remorse.

"You both know I worked for Crane, and I think we have a pretty good idea what Heidi did for a living. What's your story, Brandi?"

Brandi shrugged. "I was a federal agent who was investigating Feldspar's unauthorized use of Alaskan wolves for experiments they refused to explain to the National Wildlife Foundation. Before that I was special forces in the military. This NWF investigation was supposed to be a break from this kind of traumatic shit for me."

Ariel nodded. "Reed—the black wolf up there—talks to me in my head. He's the one they used to turn us into werewolves. Head to Wasilla, which is just a short distance from Anchorage. Reed said to look for someone named Matt. We need to get him to some sort of veterinarian too before he gets any sicker."

Look for Matthew Gray Wolf. His pack healer will be able to help me—if it's not already too late.

Ariel nodded, even though Heidi looked at her strangely. "Reed says we're looking for a Matthew Gray Wolf. A werewolf named Wolf. Gee, who's not going to figure that one out? This is some crazy shit 'B' movie we woke up in."

Brandi chuckled. "Whatever they put in your shots must have been better stuff than what I got. You're a lot sassier than the stoic scientist who kept asking all those serious questions yesterday. If I hadn't been strapped down, I'd have stuffed something into your mouth to shut you up. I really didn't want to hear what was happening to us. I wanted my death and I wanted it done quickly. They took me down with a tranquilizer gun when they caught me. I'm still too pissed to talk about it."

Ariel sighed. "My default setting is to gather information. I suppose what they did to me could have affected my personality as well as my molecular structure. Killing those two men didn't even begin to satisfy the urges I had about doing stuff to them. My entire being is on fire every second now. My wolf is there at the edge of the fire just waiting to be let loose."

"I don't want to fight anyone, but I would definitely like to spend time with two or three men. I woke up incredibly horny, and it's as bad in human form as it was in the wolf," Heidi declared.

"I feel a burning need for sex too," Ariel said. Her gaze went to their driver. "How about you, Brandi?"

"I'd jump on anything with two legs and a big Johnson. And I don't even like sex. This isn't normal arousal. This shit is going to drive me crazy soon if I don't get some. I have never had this problem in my entire life."

Ariel nodded and sighed. "The urgent need to have sex is probably part of our change. Our hormones must be running high. When Reed comes back around, I'll ask him about it. In the meantime, it shouldn't be too hard to get the fire put out where we're going. Until I do some research though, make sure the guy uses a condom and don't kiss him. We can't afford to exchange fluids and give away our nanos. That's what was in the first shot we got. If you think the change to wolf and back hurts now, I bet it's nothing compared to trying it without the nanos fixing you each time it happens."

Thanks for reading this excerpt!

For more information, visit www.donnamcdonaldauthor.com ##

BOOK LISTS (IN CORRECT READING ORDER)

HOT DAMNED SERIES
Fashionably Dead
Fashionably Dead Down Under
Hell on Heels
Fashionably Dead in Diapers
Fashionably Dead Christmas
Fashionably Hotter Than Hell

SHIFT HAPPENS SERIES
Ready to Were
Some Were in Time

MAGIC AND MAYHEM SERIES
Switching Hour
Witch Glitch
A Witch In Time

HANDCUFFS AND HAPPILY EVER AFTERS SERIES
How Hard Can it Be?
Size Matters
Cop a Feel

ABOUT ROBYN PETERMAN

Robyn Peterman writes because the people inside her head won't leave her alone until she gives them life on paper.

Her addictions include laughing really hard with friends, shoes (the expensive kind), Target, Coke Zero Cherry with extra ice in a Styrofoam cup, bejeweled reading glasses, her kids, her super-hot hubby and collecting stray animals.

A former professional actress with Broadway, film and T.V. credits, she now lives in the South with her family and too many animals to count.

Writing gives her peace and makes her whole, plus having a job where you can work in your underpants works really well for her. You can leave Robyn a message via the Contact Page and she'll get back to you as soon as her bizarre life permits! She loves to hear from her fans!

Made in the USA
Columbia, SC
27 June 2017